P9-BIG-300

3 1833 02??? ????

Fiction
Ardizzone, Tony.
Taking it home

Sunsinger Books

*Illinois Short Fiction*

*A list of books in the series appears at the back of the book.*

# Taking It Home

## Stories from the Neighborhood

## Tony Ardizzone

University of Illinois Press
Urbana and Chicago

Publication of this book was supported by a grant
from the Illinois Arts Council, a state agency.

© 1996 by Tony Ardizzone
Manufactured in the United States of America
P  5  4  3  2  1

*This book is printed on acid-free paper.*

Library of Congress Cataloging-in-Publication Data
Ardizzone, Tony.
  Taking it home : stories from the neighborhood / Tony Ardizzone.
    p.    cm. — (Sunsinger Books/Illinois short fiction)
  ISBN 0–252–06483–6 (pbk. : alk. paper)
  I. Title.   II. Series.
PS3551.R395T34   1996
813'.54 — dc20                              95–11027
                                              CIP

*again for Diane Kondrat*
*and for my teachers:*
*Daniel Curley*
*Paul Friedman, Kierker Quinn*
*George Scouffas, Mark Costello*
*Michael Anania, John Frederick Nims*
*Philip F. O'Connor, Robert Early*
*John Clellon Holmes*

So so-long and goodbye,

City of the red mesh hose and the shoulder-bag-

    banging-your-hip

It's all right with me if you forget my name—

You can't be expected to remember *every* trick—

Only try to remember that I didn't pretend

To love you for anything you were not.


And I, in turn, will remember

That once, long ago, you were the doll of the world.

And I was proud to sleep in your tireless arms.

                 —Nelson Algren

# Contents

# *Acknowledgments*

Some of these stories first appeared, in a slightly different form, in the following magazines:

*Beloit Fiction Journal, Black Warrior Review, Carolina Quarterly, Chariton Review, Descant, Epoch, Memphis State Review, Quarterly West, Seattle Review, Texas Quarterly,* and *TriQuarterly,* a publication of Northwestern University.

*Taking It Home*

# Baseball Fever

Because just as the game has its men in black who call the balls and strikes, the fairs and fouls, the safes and outs, so my life has its crew of women dressed in black hoods, floor-length black robes cinched by beads, and oversized white bow ties. The Sisters of Christian Charity, to whom I was delivered at age six by my well-meaning parents for instruction and the salvation of my eternal soul. Imagine the toughest Marlboro cowboy driving the naive calf from its mother's shadow and then roping it, tying off its hooves, drawing out from the Pentecostal flames of the campfire the red-hot brands of Guilt and Fear, and then burning the calf's hide while it writhes and squeals like one of the Three Little Piggies being devoured by the Big Bad Wolf and you have a fairly accurate picture of my life's early religious education.

I believed them when they said that what they were doing was for our own good. I believed them when they collected our monthly tuition envelopes and said it was our parents' highest duty, the very least our folks could do.

I believed them when they taught us that Protestants were misguided (led by a doubting lunatic, they refused to worship the Virgin or believe in confession, the nuns would hiss), that Jews were worldly (they were looking for a material king, Heaven on earth), that all atheists and agnostics were eternally damned (their downfall was their senseless egotism). After we were introduced to world geography I learned there were Muslims, Hindus, Buddhists, pagans, naked backward heathens—a myriad of wrong-minded religions and ways—popping off the inflated plastic globe with souls as starving for God's True Word as the broom-thin children with their hands out pictured in the ads for CARE.

My parents told me only to do as I was told. To learn, to obey, not to waste all the advantages I had. After all, they continually reminded me, I was the first of both of their families to be born in this great country. I carried the weight of expectation of all the Bacigalupos, all the Paradisos. So I'd better not screw up.

My mother took me with her to Mass every Sunday. She was partial to rear, side-aisle pews, where she'd kneel and say several rosaries, ignoring everything else that went on except Holy Communion, which she'd receive with so much reverence and humility that I'd worry she'd levitate and never return to her normal self. After each Mass we'd light a candle beneath the statue of the sad-eyed Madonna. "For special intentions," my ma would always say, then pat her always-pregnant stomach.

My father hit the pews with us on Christmas Eve and Easter Sunday, the only times other than weddings or funerals he ever wore a tie. He'd watch everyone and everything, turning like a top, now and then sucking his teeth, and didn't seem to know when to kneel or stand or cross himself. He never said any of the Latin responses. He never cracked a hymnbook and sang. He never stood and followed my mother in the line for Holy Communion. "I eat my own bread," he'd whisper as she'd try to pull him after her into the aisle. Then he'd add loudly, "Lucia, don't argue."

I didn't argue either. I concluded I'd eat my own bread too when I was old enough. In the meantime I'd be a good kid and not waste their hard-earned tuition money and learn and try to please my ma.

So I learned. Not that the earth is flat or that the four humours govern physical size and personality, but that way up in the sky is Heaven, a supposedly wonderful place full of clouds thick enough to stand on, saucers of light behind everyone's head, God's magnificent throne, and twenty-four-hour-a-day genuflecting.

I could think of several places I'd rather spend eternity (Wrigley Field, Lincoln Park Zoo, Riverview, any playground with monkey bars and unbroken swings, even the old sofa in front of Aunt Lena's black-and-white TV), but the Sisters told us our choices were Heaven, Hell, or Purgatory—no substitutions. Hell and Purgatory were made up of fires so hot you got a headache just thinking about them. The heat was worse than a glowing waffle iron, the nuns reminded us every week, so intense that the flames boiled and bubbled the miserable marrow inside your bones. In Hell even the nails of your two little fingers screamed with agony. And you'd have to stay there with nothing to do but suffer for longer than any teacher was able to count. For more years than there are grains of sand on all of the world's shores and beaches, and that wouldn't even be the first hundredth of the first second of time, which would never end because it was eternal.

During some of these "Exactly How Bad Is Hell?" lectures, my little classmates actually peed their uniform skirts or regulation navy-blue parish pants, prompting Sister to put the gory details on hold and call for the janitor and his broom and pan and bucket of sawdust.

Thanks for cluing me in, I'd think as the janitor muttered to me how I should be ashamed, how I was a big second grader. "Daniel," Sister told me, "try and sit still and perhaps your clothing will be dry by lunchtime." I nodded, then stared at my desk top. See, I was grateful. God punished bad people whether they knew about Hell or not, and Sister was giving me a lifetime of advanced warning. I'd grow up and be a very good person, I promised God. I figured you had to be really evil to end up in Hell. Hell was for people like Adolf Hitler.

But then the good Sisters pulled the old hidden-ball trick on us, and all of us smug little snotnoses were caught flat-footed, a mile off base. Because, the nuns informed us, even though we were barely able to cross Clark Street with the aid of a green light and two patrol boys, all of us had *already earned* Hell's hottest flames, all because of two people we hadn't even met.

Let's pencil in Adam and Eve, the moronic apple eaters. They had a fantastic thing going (the Garden of Eden, tons better than Heaven by the way the nuns described it), but then couldn't resist listening to the talking snake. They had to go and nibble the forbidden fruit, in the process blowing the game for the rest of us.

So God punished not only dumb Eve and Adam but everyone else who came from their apple seeds. Which meant *everybody*, from the Chinese with their chopsticks to the Eskimos in their igloos to the Australians with their crazy boomerangs. The sin boomeranged throughout the ages. Which meant we were all brothers and sisters (momentary confusion and panic: then who will I be able to marry when I grow up?), damned to the never-ending broiler, furnace, blazing hibachi of Hell.

It didn't seem fair to me. I thought hey, hold your horses, *I* wasn't there to resist the temptation. *I* didn't get to choose. If only I'd have been there—man alive—that apple would've rotted on the tree! I might have *looked* at it once or twice, maybe nodded to the snake, thrown him a dead alley rat so I could watch him eat. I might have touched the apple with my fingertips, given it a little sniff. Maybe even put my lips, my tongue, my teeth . . .

I'd have eaten it too.

I realized then that I was one of the lucky souls. I knew the truth. Plus I had a bona fide Catholic baptism stamped on my forehead. For at least a week I did my chores around the house without my ma having to tell me twice.

She was right, I concluded. You should eat God's bread. Kneeling next to her in church, I'd think of little pagans exactly my age all over the world who'd never even heard of original sin. How, when they died, their tiny heathen hands and screaming fingernails would crackle like slices of bacon in my ma's cast-iron frying pan. I'll travel all over the world when I grow up, I thought. I'll carry a hundred canteens of holy water and baptize every pagan I meet, even if I have to wrestle them first down to the ground. "It's good for you, honest, no fooling," I'd tell them. They'd be grateful to me later on. They'd shake my hand and thank me when they saw me again up in Heaven.

The missionary life was extremely attractive to me. As long as you watched out for cannibals and Communists, and didn't step on or listen to talking snakes, going around sprinkling water on heathen foreheads seemed just about the surest way to keep your buns out of the incinerator.

The nuns cushioned the Fall of humanity with another story, the Fall of the angels. It seems that trillions of years before Paradise some of God's finest archangels and seraphim were disobedient too. The good Lord was on them in a millisecond. Also he had several legions of good archangels (my first lesson in the concept of a deep bench) waiting with drawn swords behind him. The defeated lay at his ankles, gasping. God unplugged their halos, plucked their feathers, stripped them of their mighty wings. Then he stepped on a giant pedal that opened a yawning trapdoor in the clouds and all of the militant angels tumbled down from the blue sky.

In that moment of eternity's early timelessness, it rained angels—it rained devils—and they plummeted through space with a moan: like falling meteors, comets, Skylabs, Cosmos 1402s, twisting in an everlasting sizzle as the eager tongues of Hell's waiting fires leapt past their cloven feet to their devil mouths and French-kissed them.

This was the creation of Hell. Wowee! we all thought.

Indirectly these stories also taught us a lot about this strange being we called God. For one, he wasn't a father who took much sass. Also he didn't seem to give second chances. (We didn't get to the New Testament until third grade.) God was all-powerful and knew and saw everything, everywhere, always; and to top it off he was invisible. Ogres in the Brothers Grimm seemed more benign.

What choice did we have? We could hardly raise our trembling hands and ask Sister to tell us a different fairy tale. This, the stern women in black were teaching us, was for real. Each year for eight years the well-meaning Sisters of Christian Charity trotted out these horror stories, and each year for eight years I listened with increasing fear.

We were told that, as Adam swallowed, the lump of apple caught in his throat and remained there, a constant reminder of our sinful, evil nature. We were told that the talking serpent still slithers through the world in the form of creeping communism. All we had to do was ask our fathers to read us the newspaper; President Ike was combating it every day. One of the statues in our classroom showed Mary stepping on the writhing serpent. "See?" the nun would say. It was all the proof we needed. Evil was in our throats, in our world, even under the foot of the Blessed Virgin. Evil was everywhere. After the flames kissed them, the evil angels escaped from Hell and worked their way up to the earth, where they walk our streets and alleys, always in disguise, always looking like normal people, always there behind a street-light pole or the open door of a strange car, hoping to lead us into the darkness of despair, into temptation, occasions of sin, eternal everlasting damnation.

I should tell you that my number is 13, so you'll recognize me down on the field. Every team from high school on gladly allowed me to wear it. No one else wanted 13 but me. Because when baseball collided with Mickey's death and I was forced to abandon my dreams of becoming a missionary, I felt it was only right and proper that the rest of my playing days be spent in sheer defiance of misfortune.

Because the first of our line of Paradisos and Bacigalupos to be born into the nation of baseball earned his birthright and stepped right out of Paradise into the foul mouth of the wolf.

Because I believed the good Sisters when they said that at seven you tag the age of reason, that from the moment the candles on your birthday cake go out everything you do goes into the record book. Because at age eight I was involved in a very extraordinary, extremely tragic play. I wish I could say it was a bit part in a grammar-school production of *Macbeth* or *Hamlet*. It wasn't. It was purple-faced, bulging-eyes real.

I didn't want to be evil and re-earn Hell, but if you've got the genes of a natural-born ballplayer it's not easy to pass up a fat pitch.

So I went with the pitch that began my life as a ballplayer.

\* \* \*

On the city's North Side, on a street named Olive, in the middle of a solid neighborhood of working-class Irish and Germans and Poles, with a few Italian families like mine sprinkled here and there, like basil, for flavor. Everyone lived in gray or red brick two-flats. Upstairs lived the tenants, preferably old people who didn't smell and who treaded the hallway quietly. The front of every house had a porch that faced a tree. Everybody except the old people and the Meenans and the Jankowskis had a new baby every year or so. At first we babies stumbled around our tiny backyards, eating grass and twigs and pebbles too large to stick in our nostrils and crunchy paint chips from the wooden garages that opened into the *stay away from there, do you hear me!* alley, touching fingers through the tilted square gaps in our chain-link fences that separated us, careful not to trample our fathers' tomato plants. Then we were promoted to the front yards, where we were yelled at by everyone. Because the new open space turned us into a herd of stampeding buffalo, and everyone had just planted marigolds or snapdragons or new grass seed. Perhaps because they were trained to be dainty, the girls at once obeyed. But we boys had no control over our shoes. So we fled and graduated ourselves to the alley.

The girls stayed in the front yards because they said the alley wasn't clean. Really they were afraid of the rats you would see sometimes munching on the day's garbage that spilled out of the big oil drums each house kept alongside its alley gate. Humor-

less men from the rodent-control section of the city's board of
health marched through every spring stapling signs to the telephone poles:

WARNING!
THIS BLOCK HAS BEEN BAITED
WITH RED SQUILL AND WARFARIN

So we called ourselves the Rat Squill Warfarins and armed
ourselves with fifth-grader Joey Petrovich's baseball bat, and the
alley became our kingdom, our playground, our limestone-and-
asphalt Garden of Eden.

We explored every inch of it, naming every garbage can (Blue
Streak, Rusty, Triple Dent), garage door (Big Ben, Lucky Green,
Smasharoo), backyard gate (Squeaky, Busted Man, Fort Coman-
che). In the front yards our sisters stepped around the nodding
petunias and drew squares on the ratless sidewalk with pieces
of colored chalk. They began wearing dresses, barrettes, and red
rubber bands to hold back their long hair. From our knees in the
alley we could hear them sing.

*"I live on Ol-live!"*

Over and over and over, until we thought we'd go mad.

*"Ay lives on Ol-live!*
*Ee lives on Ol-live!*
*I live on Ol-live!*
*Oh lives on Ol-live!*
*Do you live on Ol-live?"*

And they always sang *see wye see oh?* (can you come out?)
when they called from the backyards to one another to come out
to play. I'd hear my sisters Rosaria and Tina. I'd listen, tempted
to open my mouth and sing *en wye* (not yet) or *eye ay ell double
you* (in a little while). But we were Rat Squill Warfarins; our rules

said you couldn't sing. Our voices might scare away the rats that we hunted with rocks and Joey's baseball bat.

Whenever it rained or when one of our fathers would unroll his green garden hose and soap down his car, the potholes in our alley would brim deliciously with water and our playground would become the Chain of Great Lakes. We would play Dams and Beavers, on our hands and knees, using stones and sticks and pieces of broken glass. We'd see which one of us had the biggest beaver's buck teeth. Then Joey Petrovich's dark eyes would twinkle and he'd play Dive Bomber and smash our dams with his bat.

HOMES, Frankie Biermann taught us. Huron, Ontario, Michigan, Erie, Superior. Frankie had blond hair and polio and a brace on one leg. When you asked him if he had polio he said, "Yeah, that's how come my middle leg's so short." Skeeter Egan, who always wore his hair in a flattop and who could run faster than Old Lady Misiak's alley cat, and whose twin sister Deirdre was the most beautiful girl in the world, said Superior was the best.

Then for a while it didn't rain, and everyone's father's car was clean, and everything had a name, and the rats had made themselves so scarce that we forgot all about them. Then Lenny Sakowicz, whose arm muscles were as hard as cue balls, got a baseball and a genuine autographed mitt, and we all begged our parents for mitts. After my father told me no, "Don't be stupid, Danilo, I'll slap you, don't even ask," I got the scissors from the pantry and cut out all the pictures of baseball gloves in the Sears and Montgomery Wards catalogues my mother kept in a drawer in the china cabinet, and every night I'd stick one with my spit to the bathroom mirror, where he'd see it the next morning when he shaved. Each morning when I woke to go to school I'd find my mitt floating in the toilet bowl. Dive bomber, I'd think as I'd sink the bit of paper with my pee.

But enough of the other kids got gloves. Then Joey and Lenny created the Olive Street Alley League, and Frankie got a pencil and wrote all of the rules down.

*Hitters gitters* was the first commandment. That included even the backyards of childless old people who owned fierce dogs. *Ricochets are fair in play* was commandment number two. Off a garage roof was foul. Off telephone wires, fair. Pitcher's hands, you're out of there. Break somebody's window and everybody runs, with the hitter responsible for picking up the bat. Joey and the big guys foresaw most, but not all, of the possibilities.

"This here's a league of line-drive sluggers," the big guys said.

"Line-drive sluggos," echoed all of us little guys, even Frankie Biermann, whose leg brace made it awful hard for him to run.

Mickey Meenan was a very quiet kid, and most of the time he was around you didn't even notice he was there. He was tall for a third grader, gawky, spotted everywhere you could see with freckles, and he'd pick his earwax with his little finger or a stick and then stare at it for so long he made you ask him what was he going to do with it. "I dunno," he'd always say, and then he'd always eat it or wipe it on his pants leg and then start working on his other ear. All the kids thought he was spoiled because he was an only child. Really, we were jealous. Mickey had a hundred toys, none of them broken; a thousand comic books, not one page torn.

Other than Grace Jankowski, in our neighborhood of mostly Catholic families Mickey was the only only child. Even though he was Catholic, his parents sent him to the public school on Bryn Mawr. So he was doubly strange.

Mickey's father had a job with the city, sleeping in trucks parked along the street where they had big potholes or busted water pipes, and he'd let us gather inside his garage as he'd boast that his CAUTION MEN WORKING signs sweated more in summer than he did. He was a big man and always smoked a fat cigar, and he'd tell us how great it was to go up to Wisconsin to shoot birds, really blast them out of the sky, or blow little squirrels or bunny rabbits to smithereens, and then he'd take out his shotgun and put a finger to his lips and say, "Shhh, be vewy vewy quiet. I'm hunting wabbits." We'd clap our hands with glee. Then he'd tell us how he'd once been a professional boxer, though he quit before he got cauliflower ears. He'd let us look at his ears, and we'd beg him to do Elmer Fudd again, and he'd say he was pleased as punch we played with his kid, and then he'd grab Mickey and rub his head real hard with his knuckles. Mickey would say nothing, except his face got fire-truck red as he squirmed.

Sometimes we'd tease Mickey about eating earwax and being spoiled, until he invited all of us over to his house. Mrs. Meenan made a hundred oatmeal cookies and ten gallons of Wyler's lemonade, and Joey and Lenny swiped a bunch of comics, and Frankie fell on a couple of toys and broke them all to pieces, and Mr. Meenan laughed and laughed and stunk up the house with his cigar, and everybody but poor Mickey had a wonderful time.

It was an accident, and it happened before I could even drop the bat and run. Winky Winkler danced on second base. Mickey was playing the garage door just behind first. It was a Saturday in early April and we had planned a triple-header, and we were getting good because several of us had our timing down.

Because it was a league of line-drive sluggos.

The ball cracked off the bat and I started to drop it as I ran toward first base, but I heard a hollow squish and Mickey stood there by Lucky Green staring right at me with no expression on his face. Then the world stopped as his bulbs went dim and he fell to his knees. For half a second I thought it was just a joke; I thought that Mickey had suddenly been struck by a sense of humor, that he'd begin to pray in pig Latin or sing "I live on Ol-live!" or crawl like a turtle toward the ball. I wanted him to pick the ball up because I knew I could beat his throw. I wanted him to stand. I wanted him to say *something.*

Because suddenly I was terribly afraid.

By the time we got to him he had fallen to his face. Then Lenny and Joey and the rest of the guys rolled him over. His face and neck were turning blue. His throat was trying to pronounce the letter *K.* His eyes looked backward into his head.

"You're all right, Meenan," everybody said.

"Right off his Adam's apple! Didja see it?"

"Wake him up."

"Get the smelling salts."

"You shoulda seen it! It looked like he was trying to eat the ball!"

"You're OK, Meenan."

"Get up, sluggo."

"You killed him, 'Galupo. Honest to Jesus!"

"He ain't even breathing."

We got him under his armpits and tried to make him walk. "You're all right, Meenan." His feet dragged like a Raggedy Andy doll. "Honest, Danny, I bet you killed him." Some of the guys laughed, scared and nervous. Little Frankie Biermann looked like he was going to cry. Then somebody took off down the alley toward Mickey's house. "Take deep breaths, Meenan, you're OK, you're OK." He wasn't very heavy. His skin still felt warm. His head rolled on his chest like Mr. Sakowicz's on Friday nights when the men from the foundry walked him home drunk.

Mrs. Meenan bawled over Mickey as she knelt on her front-yard grass. We waited for the ambulance. I thought I could hear the trees above me whisper their name. "Meenan," the leaves in the wind whispered. Then somebody shouted, "Hey Danny, better make yourself scarce."

There are times when events overload your circuits, and inside you blow a fuse. Your head suddenly goes dark. Dad says, "Lucy, where the hell did I put that goddamn flashlight?" You help him as he walks down into the basement, thinking maybe you'll get lucky and see a rat, hearing the sudden roar of the furnace as it kicks in. The sound frightens you but you're with your dad. Yet he says nothing as he shines his flashlight, the only light in the world, on the gray fuse box.

"Say something to him, Francis."

"Get me a clean shirt. I have to shave."

"Again?"

"I can't go over there wearing this filthy shirt."

Supper, some soup and noodles, and nobody talked until Louie started to sniffle, then cry. Mamma held Francis Junior and said, "Eat." Only the baby ate, one hand raised and wrapped in Ma's dark curly hair, the other holding her breast so she wouldn't pull it away. The rest of us sat around the table, not eating. Louie wiped his tears with the fist that held his spoon. Dominic poked his noodles with his fingertips. Gino stared up at the ceiling, making stupid sounds with his tongue, and Tina held her rubber doll just like Mamma held Francis Junior. Rosaria's hands hid her face. I looked at their dark heads, then down at my soup, then at the little piece of bloodstained toilet paper Dad had clinging to his chin, then at the dish towel he wore over his immaculate white shirt.

Mamma thought I was asleep when they came back from their visit to the Meenans that night. Everybody was in bed. She kissed the others, then touched my forehead with her hand, pressing the coolness of her palm against me for several moments. Now I realize that she most likely said a prayer, that she meant the touch to be comforting, reassuring. But it confused me then. I couldn't understand why she didn't bend down to kiss me until the middle of the night, when sound-asleep Louie woke me by peeing out his misery against my leg.

She didn't kiss me, I thought, because my forehead now had the mark of Cain, and even in the darkness my own mother could see it.

I'll run away, I thought. I imagined myself as a hobo with a burnt-cork Halloween beard, a stick over my shoulder, and all my belongings inside a red bandanna, riding the rails to the Wild West's unknown frontiers, my leg eternally wet with my brother's pee.

The next day I escaped, just before I could be taken to church. Ma was busy changing Francis Junior's diapers. Dad shaved in the bathroom. I scooted out the back door and ran to the Bryn Mawr El station, slipping under the turnstile and jumping on the first passing train, which happened to be going south. I was terrified when the cars dipped into the dark tunnel just beyond Fullerton. I thought the El was always elevated. I feared that God was sending me down to Hell. But then the ride leveled off. I rode that train until I was the only white person on board, then got off, somewhere on the South Side. I took the next train that stopped at the platform, riding north to Howard Street, the end of the line.

Then I went back south, plunging deeper, no longer afraid of the tunnel or of being the only white. People were friendly to me. "Where you going, boy?" they asked. "Say, you lost?" I pretended that I couldn't speak, pointing to my mouth and shaking my head no. "You must be one of them deaf-mutes." I nodded yes and smiled. An old woman gave me a stick of peppermint gum.

I rode back and forth most of that Sunday. I don't know why I finally went home. No one said a word to me about my absence. At my place at the kitchen table there was an empty plate, a fork, a spoon. My ma looked like she wanted to ask me where I'd been all day, but my father's silence made the house too heavy for her or anyone to talk.

And then I became so sick that the doctor had to quarantine the house. I didn't fall sick with scarlet fever because I'd murdered Mickey Meenan, though at the time I was convinced that was why. I fell ill because I inhaled streptococci in one of those El cars, and a legion of homeless scarlet-fever bees built a hive inside my heart. Then the bees' bubbling honey leaked into my bloodstream and fried my cheeks, my legs, my bones. My guts flamed. Everywhere I was aching hot. Thrashing on the sweat-soaked sheets of my parents' double bed, I boiled like a lobster inside the steaming pot of my skin.

The parish priest wouldn't come to the house to bless me because of the quarantine. My mother rinsed my forehead and chest with holy water she pilfered from the vestibule. She filled the bedroom with a hundred red votive candles that flickered everywhere I could see, and then the room grew dozens of stand-by-themselves crucifixes, and three times each day my brothers and sisters knelt outside my closed door and recited the rosary and the Litany for the Dead. *Oh Lord, deliver them. We beseech thee, hear us.* I ate ice cubes made of water and red wine. When I could I peed into a soup pot. My ma brought every vigil candle on the North Side into that room, and after each rosary and litany she cracked the door open and tiptoed in and had me kiss the feet, hands, side, and head of each of the crucifixes that stood behind the tiers of bouncing candles and hung on my sickroom's four walls.

You'd think I would have lain on my damp sheets praying for the eternal salvation of my wretched soul and for eternal rest for the dearly departed Mickey Meenan. You'd think the words *I'm so sorry, dearest God* would have been starters in the lineup on my lips. They weren't even on the team. My mind and soul sang a different cha-cha.

"My little sister Tina could've gotten out of the way of that liner, dear God. You know I ain't lying. So why couldn't you have let the spaz catch it? Or at least made him duck? A dog would have known enough to duck. You make the pigeons fly away when the ball goes near them. So how come it didn't work with Meenan? You can do *anything*, remember? You could have let it ricochet off his forehead. Given the kid a shiner. Busted his nose. Knocked out his two front teeth. Why'd you have to let me kill him? Our Father, who art in Heaven, what you let happen couldn't have been worse! All right, so maybe you really needed him up there in Heaven for some strange and mysterious reason. In school Sister's all the time telling us that's the way you like to operate. But you could have killed him a million other ways! You could have let him catch rabies from one of the alley rats! Why me? What did I ever do? *What did I ever do?*"

While my family knelt in the hallway outside my door, respectfully slurring *the Lord is with thee* and *blessed is the fruit of thy womb.*

I thought a lot about Hell. I'd let my fever work itself up until

I felt I was made of fire, and then I'd squint at the endless rows of candles. The flames would shimmy in their little cups and I'd see a dancing sea of red. I'd pretend it was a glimpse of Hell, and I was just outside, in one of Hell's waiting rooms, about to receive my punishment. I'd try to imagine eternity and begin to multiply two times two times two times two until the numbers melted in my brain. Sometimes I'd pull myself to the bed's edge and reach out and stick my little finger into one of the flames. I'd try to hold my finger there, the multiplication tables hovering on my lips, but my arm always pulled my hand back. Then I'd feel my forehead for my mark of Cain and lie back on my pillow, exhausted.

I'd play a game with the crucifixes. If I lay perfectly still there was always at least one Jesus whose hollow cheeks reflected the flames in a way that made his head move. I'd stare at that Jesus and ask him questions.

"Are you happy hanging on your cross?"

No, his head would shake.

"Is Meenan still alive?"

Again, no.

"Will I be well in time to make my First Holy Communion?"

No.

"Does anybody love me?"

No.

"When I die, will I go to Heaven?"

Always no, no, no.

"Then stay on your old cross," I'd whisper, then feel terrible and cry until my tears made little puddles in my ears.

I'd think of baseballs, endlessly arcing in on me, my hands gripping the bat, my wrists snapping the sweet part against the lazy ball. I played more games in my head than convents have black shoes and stockings. In every one I always hit safe line drives that were at least fifty feet over every fielder's head, that sailed like kite strings through the air, touching nothing, nothing, ever. Never old Adam's forbidden apple stuck in an innocent freckled kid's throat. No, my balls would always land with a magnificent splash in the middle of Lakes Huron, Ontario, Michigan, Erie, and Superior.

Only when the fat doctor came to probe me with his instruments would the room fill with blinding light. I imagined him as Satan's chief inspector trying to decide which boiler room I'd be sentenced to and how high to set the thermostat. "His fever hasn't broken yet," he'd say. "Let's give it some more time." Then he'd turn with a belch or a fart, and my ma would sigh and turn off the terrible light, then replace the spent candles, then call the little disciples to the hallway for the evening's rosary and litany, which was followed by another round of sacred wound kissing.

Meanwhile my former classmates shuffled through practice and then real confession en route to their first-Sunday-in-May march up to the Eternal Bread Line. "So what if I miss making First Holy Spumoni?" I hissed at the flickering flames. I was sick of being sick and so jealous I wouldn't be with them that I wished none of them would have any fun. I prayed the monsignor would screw up and none of the Sacred Snacks would get consecrated. "No, no, no," said the Jesus with the moving head.

I pictured the church, glowing more greenly than kryptonite, as the priest topped each communicant's virgin tongue. I imagined their sin-free souls gleaming like my feet in the X-ray machine at Maury's Bargain Shoe Store. I saw the ribboned pews and kneelers. All the kids filling their chipmunk cheeks with Christ. Everyone afterward posing on the church steps for adorable snapshots. Then they'd all tumble like socks in a dryer into a hundred just-washed Fords and Chevies, happily driving home to hamburgers on the grill, reheated roast beef, pineapple-covered ham, white First Communion cake. And all of them knowing why I, the little murderer nailed to the cross of scarlet fever, wasn't there.

By then I was able to sit up and not feel woozy, and that afternoon I held the wall and slid my feet to the window, then pushed apart the dusty drapes and pulled up one narrow yellow slat of the venetian blinds. I was able to gaze out on a sunny sliver of Olive Street, so I stayed there, dizzily holding on to the drapes, until Mr. Egan's pine-green Plymouth scraped its whitewalls against the curb and Skeeter bounded out of the backseat in his white suit and bow tie. Sanctifying grace beamed all over his face. He twirled his thick Communion candle like a baton. Then Deirdre slid from the car like an angel on Christmas morning. I cried then, if my body had enough liquid left in it to cry. I began knocking down the rows of crucifixes and blowing out the thousand candles. It felt like a cruel birthday party I hadn't been invited to, and since I couldn't blow out all the candles with one breath, I realized that I wouldn't get my wish.

Which wasn't that the liner had never left my bat or if it had that it hadn't struck Mickey or that Mickey could be resurrected. I was more selfish than that. My wish was that I could be *normal* again.

Because I'd seen what happened to the kids who weren't. The others ganged up on them like a school of pet-store piranhas. They took chunks out of you until you were barely alive. They tripped you whenever you tried to walk down their row. They stuck KICK ME I'M AN ASSHOLE signs on your back with chewing gum. They snotted out gobs of boogers on your seat, then hooted like hyenas when you sat in it. They hid Tootsie Rolls of dog shit in your desk. No one would sit with you in the lunch room, mess around with you out on the playground, stand next to you when you waited in line.

So I blew out every one of the damn candles and kicked over the soup pot and then got up on a chair so I could take all the crucifixes down from the walls when my ma came in and screamed, "Francis, Gino, Dominic, Rosaria, Tina, Louie, Francis Junior! Thank God! Our prayers are answered! Danny's well!"

And, in a way, I was.

# Nonna

She has seen it all change.

Follow her now as she walks slowly down Loomis toward Taylor, her heavy black purse dangling at her side. Though it is the middle of summer she wears her black overcoat. The air conditioning is too cold inside the stores, she thinks. But the woman is not sure she is outside today to do her shopping. It is afternoon, and on summer afternoons she walks. She walks to escape the stifling heat of her tiny apartment, the thick drapes drawn shut to shade her two rooms from the sun, the air flat and silent, except for the ticking of her clock. Walking is good for her blood, she believes. Like eating the cloves of *aglio*.

She hesitates, the sharp taste of *aglio* on her tongue. Perhaps she is outside this afternoon to shop. She cannot decide. The children of the old neighborhood call out to her as she passes them. *Na-na!* The sound used to call in goats. Or, sometimes, to tease. Or is it *Nonna*, grandmother, that they call? It makes no difference, the woman thinks. The thin-ribbed city dogs sniff the hem of her long black dress, wagging their dark tails against her legs. Crickets call from a clump of weeds. Sparrows flit above her head.

Around her is the bustle of the street corner, the steady rumble and jounce of cars and delivery trucks, the fiercely honking horns, the long screeching hiss of a braking CTA bus. The young men from the Taylor Street Social and Athletic Club ignore her as she passes. They lean against streetlight poles and parking meters in the hot afternoon sun. One chews a cigar; another, a toothpick. One struts in front of her, then turns to the gutter and spits. The woman looks into their faces but does not recognize any of them, even though she knows they are the sons of the sons of the neighborhood men she and Vincenzo once knew. Grandsons of *com-*

*pari*. Do they speak the old language? she wonders. Like a young girl, she is too shy to ask them.

One boy wears a cornicelli and a thin cross around his neck. The golden horn and cross sparkle in the light. Nonna squints. Well, she thinks, at least they are still Catholic, and her lips move as she says to herself, *They are still Catholics,* and her hand begins to form the sign of the cross. Then she remembers she is out on the street, so she stops herself. Some things are better done privately. The boy's muscled arms are dark, tanned, folded gracefully over his sleeveless undershirt. The boy has a strong chin. Nonna smiles and wets her lips in anticipation of greeting this handsome boy but his eyes stare past her, vacantly, at the rutted potholes and assorted litter lying alongside the curb in the street.

She looks at what he stares at. He grunts to himself and joins his friends. Across the street, on the shaded side of Loomis, is the new store, a bookstore. The letters above the front window read T SWANKS. Could the *T* stand for Tonio? she wonders. She crosses the street. Then it should properly be an *A*. For Antonio. Anthony. Named for any one of the many holy Antonios, maybe even for the gentle Francescano from Padova. Nonna always preferred the Franciscan but never told anyone. He had helped her to find many lost things. She believes that if she were to speak her preference aloud she would give offense to all the others, and what does she know of them? Heaven is full of marvelous saints. Her lips whisper *Padova*.

The sound is light. Nonna enjoys it and smiles. She pictures Padova on the worn, tired boot. Vincenzo used to call Italy that. Nonna recalls that Padova sits far up in the north, west of Venezia. She looks down at her black shoes. Italia. She came from the south, from Napoli, and Vincenzo, her husband, may he rest, came from the town of Altofonte, near Palermo, in Sicilia. The good strong second son of *contadini*.

A placard in the bookstore window reads FREE TEA OR COF-FEE—BROWSERS WELCOME. Nonna whispers the words. She is tempted to enter. She draws together the flaps of her heavy coat. She could look at a map of Italy if the store has a book of maps, and then maybe she could ask Mr. Swanks for which of the holy Antonios was he named. And what part of the boot his family came from, and does he still speak the old language? She does not realize that T. Swanks might not be the name of the store's proprietor. She assumes that, like many, Swanks is an Italian who has shortened his name.

Beneath the sign in the window stands a chess set. Its pieces seem made of ivory. The woman stares at the tiny white horse. It resembles bone. She remembers the evening she and Vincenzo were out walking in the fields and came across a skeleton. That was in New Jersey, where they had met, before they came to Chicago. She thought the skeleton was a young child's—she flailed her arms and screamed—but then Vincenzo held her hands and assured her it was only an animal. Eh, a dog or a lamb, he had said, his thin face smiling. Digging with his shoe, Vincenzo then uncovered the carcass. It indeed had looked like a dog or a lamb. That was a night she would never forget, the woman thinks. And that smell. *Dio!* It had made her young husband turn away and vomit. But Nonna is certain that what she saw in that field that dusky autumn evening had been a child, a newborn *bambino*, clothed only by a damp blanket of leaves. The devil had made it look like a dog! New Jersey was never the same after that. She begged Vincenzo to quit his job at the foundry. They had to go away from that terrible place. Nonna openly makes the sign of the cross.

She knows what she has seen. And she knows what kind of woman did it. Not a Catholic, she thinks, for that would have been the very worst of sins. It had been someone without religious training. Maybe a Mexican. But there hadn't been any Mexicans in New Jersey. Nonna is puzzled again. And all Mexicans are Catholic, she thinks. Each Sunday now the church is full of them. They sit to the one side, the Virgin's side, in the back pews. Afterward they greet one another merrily in the sun, then parade to their Mexican grocery store. And what do they buy? Nonna had wondered about that all during Mass one bright morning, and then from church she had followed them. The Mexicans came out of their strange store talking their quick Mexican and carrying bananas and bags of little flat breads. Great bunches of long bananas. So green!

Maybe Mexicans don't know how to bake with yeast. Nonna realizes that her lips are moving again, so she covers her mouth with her hand. If that is true, she thinks, then maybe she should go inside Mr. Antonio Swanks's new Italian bookstore and see if he has a book on how to use yeast. She could bring it to the Mexicans. It might make them happy. When they kneel in the rear pews, the Mexicans never look happy. Nonna shifts her weight from foot to foot, staring at the little white horse.

But the book would have to be in Mexican. And it would cost money, she thinks. She does not have much money. Barely enough for necessities, for neck bones and the beans of coffee and *formaggio* and *aglio* and salt. And of course for bread. What was she thinking about? Did she have to go to the store to buy something? Or is she just outside for her walk?

She looks inside the bookstore window and sees a long-haired girl sitting behind the counter. Her head is bent. She is reading. Nonna smiles. It is what a young girl should do when she is in a bookstore. She should study books. When she is in church she should pray for a good husband, someone young, with a job, who will not hit her. Then when she is older, married, she should pray to the Madonna for some children. To have one. To have enough. Nonna nods and begins counting on her fingers. For a moment she stops, wondering where she placed her rosary.

No, she says aloud. She is counting children, not saying the rosary.

Nonna is pleased she has remembered. It is a pleasant thought. Five children for the girl—one for each finger—and then one special child for her to hold tightly in her palm. That would be enough. They would keep the girl busy until she became an old woman, and then, if she has been a good mother, she could live with one of her sons. The girl behind the counter turns a page of her book. Nonna wonders what happened to her own children. Where were Nonna's sons?

She hears a shout from the street. She turns. A carload of boys has squealed to a stop, and now from the long red-finned automobile the boys are spilling out. Are they her sons? Nonna stares at them. The young men from the corner gather around the car's hood. One thumps his hand on the shining metal on his way to the others. One boy is laughing. She sees his white teeth. He embraces the other boy, then throws a mock punch.

They are not her sons.

She turns back. It is clear to her now that the girl has no children. So that is why she is praying there behind the counter! Nonna wants to go inside so she can tell the unfortunate Mrs. Swanks not to give up hope, that she is still young and healthy, that there is still time, that regardless of how it appears the holy saints are always listening, always testing, always waiting for you to throw up your hands and say *basta* and surrender so that they can say heh, we would have given you a house full of *bambini* if only you had said one more novena. Recited one more rosary. Lit one more candle. Crossed yourself one additional time. But you gave up hope.

The saints and the Madonna were like that. Time to those who've earned eternity does not mean very much. But even God knows that each woman deserves her own baby. Didn't he give even the Virgin a son?

Poor Mrs. Swanks. Her Antonio must not be good for her. It is often the fault of the man. The doctors in New Jersey had told Nonna that. Not once, but many times. That was so long ago. But do you think I listened? Nonna says to herself. For one moment? For all those years? My ears were deaf! Nonna gestures angrily with her hands. She strikes the store's glass window. It was part of Heaven's test, she is saying, to see if I would stop believing! She pulls her arms to her breasts as she notices the black horses. They stare at her with hollow eyes. Inside the store the manager closes his book and comes toward the window. Nonna watches her close the book and stand, then raise her head. She wears a moustache. It is a boy.

Nonna shuts her eyes and turns. She was thinking of something. But now she has forgotten again. She breathes through her open mouth. It was the boys, she thinks. They did something to upset her. She walks slowly now to slow her racing heart. Did they throw snowballs at her? No, it is not winter again. Nonna looks around at the street and the sidewalk. No, there is no snow. But she feels cold.

Then they must have said something again, she thinks. What was it? Something cruel. She stops on the street. Something about . . .

The word returns. *Bread.*

So she is outside to go to the bakery. Nonna smiles. It is a very good idea, she thinks, because she has no bread. She begins walking again, wondering why she has trekked all the way to Taylor Street if she was out only for bread. The Speranza Bakery is on Flournoy Street, she says aloud. Still, it is pleasant today, and walking is good for her heart. She thinks of what she might buy. A small roll to soak in her evening coffee?

The afternoon is bright. Nonna walks up the shaded side of Loomis, looking ahead like an excited child at the statue of Christopher Columbus in the park. Furry white clouds float behind the statue's head. Jets of water splash at its feet. She remembers the day the workers uncovered it. There had been a parade and many important speeches. Was there a parade now? Nonna faces the street. There is only a garbage truck.

So it must not be Columbus Day. Unless the garbage truck is leading the parade. But the mayor leads the parade, Nonna says, and the mayor is not a garbage truck. She laughs at her joke. She is enjoying herself, and she looks again at the green leaves on the trees and the clean, white clouds in the blue sky.

The mayor, she hears herself saying, is Irish. Nonna wonders why Irish is green. Italy is green too, and also red and white. The garbage truck clattering by her now is blue. So many colors.

She thinks of something but cannot place it. It is something about Italians and the Irish. The Irish mayor. His name. He cannot be *paesano* because he is not from Italy. But she knows it is something to do with that. At the curb alongside her a pigeon pecks a crushed soda can.

It is Judas. Nonna remembers everything now. How the mayor unveiled the statue and then switched on the water in the fountain, how all the people of the neighborhood cheered him when he waved to them from the street. All the police. Then the people were dark and angry, and the police had to hold them back. Where did the people want to go? Nonna thinks, then remembers. To the university, she says, to the new school of Illinois that the Irish Judas had decided to build in their neighborhood. The mayor's Judas shovel broke the dirt. Then, one by one, the old Italian stores closed, and the *compari* and *amici* boxed their belongings and moved, and the Judas trucks and bulldozers knocked down their stores and houses. The people watched from the broken sidewalk. Nonna remembers the woman who had tapped on her door, asking if she would sign the petition paper. The paper asked the mayor to leave the university where it was, out on a pier on the lake. Was that any place for a school? Nonna asked the woman. The woman then spoke to her in the old language, but in the Sicilian dialect, saying that Navy Pier was a perfectly good place. Then why build the university here? Nonna said. Daley, the woman said. Because of Mayor Richard J. Daley. Because he betrayed us. Because it seems as if he wants to destroy all that the Italians in Chicago have built. First on the North Side, when they built the Cabrini Green projects and destroyed Saint Philip

Benizi's Church, they drove us out. Now they want to do it again here. He wants to drive us entirely from his city even though we have always voted for him and supported his political machine. Sign the paper. If you understand me and agree, please sign the paper. For a moment Nonna thinks she is the woman. She looks down to see the paper in her hands.

There is no paper. The paper had not been any good. The men in the street had told Nonna that. Shouting up to her windows, waving at her with their angry fists. She'd yelled at them from her windows for them not to make so much noise. Two men tried to explain. Then what is good? Nonna has asked them. You tell me, I want to know. What is good? She is shouting. A car on Loomis slows, then passes her by and speeds up.

These, the men had answered. Rocks. Nonna is afraid again as she remembers. She'd pulled her drapes tightly shut. But still from behind her open windows she had been able to hear all through the long night the shouts of the men who kept her awake and the rocks, rocks, rocks thrown at the squad cars patrolling the streets and through the windows of the alderman's office.

She hears the water. Splashing up to the feet of Christopher Columbus, the boy who stood at the sea's edge thinking the world was round like a shiny new apple. Nonna knows history. She memorized it to pass the citizenship test. Columbus asked himself why he first saw the tall sails of approaching ships, and then the apple fell from the tree and hit him on the head, and he discovered it. Nonna is smiling. She is proud that Columbus is *paesano*. Sometimes when she studied and could not remember an answer, she would hit herself on the head. That knocks the answer out of sleeping, she says. Though sometimes it does not, and Nonna thinks of her own head, how once it had been full of answers and truths, but now many answers were no longer there. Perhaps she lost them when she wasn't looking. Should she pray to Saint Anthony? But he helps only with things, with lost objects. Maybe, Nonna thinks, when she puts something new inside her head something old must then fall out. And then it is lost forever. That makes sense, she says. She laughs to herself. It is the way it is with everything. The new pushes out the old. And then . . . She puts her hands to her head.

There is only so much here, she says. Only so many places to put the answers. Nonna thinks of the inside of her head. She pictures brains and bone and blood. Like in the round white cartons in the butcher's shop, she says. She makes a face. All those answers in all those little cartons. Suddenly Nonna is hungry. She wants a red apple.

A group of girls sits at the fountain's edge. Nonna hears their talk. She looks at them, cocking her head. Did they just ask her for an apple? Someone had just been asking her a question. I don't have any, she says to the girls. She pats the pockets of her black coat. See? she says. No apples. She wonders what kind of girls they are, to be laughing like that on the street.

They must be common, Nonna thinks. Their laughter bounces up and down the sunny avenue. Like Lucia, the girl who lives downstairs, who sometimes sits out on the steps on summer nights playing her radio. Nonna often watches the girl from her windows; how can she help it, the music is always so loud. A polite girl, Nonna thinks, but always with that radio. And once, one night when Nonna was kneeling in her front room before her statue of the Madonna, she heard Lucia with somebody below on the stairs. Nonna stopped praying and listened. She could not understand any of the words but she recognized the tone and, oh, she knew what the girl and the boy were doing. The night was hot, and that brought back to her the thin face of her Vincenzo, and she was suddenly young again and back in terrible New Jersey, in her parents' house, with young Vincenzo in the stuffed chair opposite her and around them the soft sound of her mother's fitful snoring. Nonna shakes her head. She knows what she must feel about that night. She was naive, trusting, and Vincenzo was so handsome—his black curls lay so delicately across his forehead, and his smile was so wet and so white, bright—so she allowed the young boy to sit next to her on the sofa, and she did not protest when he took her hand, and then when he kissed her she even parted her lips and let his wet tongue touch hers. Oh, she was so frightened. Her mouth had been so dry. On the street now she is trembling. She is too terrified to remember the rest. But the memory spills across her mind with the sound of the girls' easy laughter, and she moves back on the pink sofa and does not put up her hands as Vincenzo strokes her cheek and then touches her, gently, on the front of her green dress. Then she turned to the boy and quickly kissed him. The light from the oil lamp flickered. The snoring stopped. She looked at Vincenzo and blushed with the shame of her mortal sin, and now if Vincenzo does not say they will marry she knows she will have to take her own life, and that indeed in God's eyes through her sin she has already died.

Nonna is still, silent, standing in her guilt on the street, afraid even now to cross herself for fear she will be struck down. She feels the sin's stifling weight. It presses down on her like a stone. Vincenzo then moved back to the stuffed chair, coughing. Neither spoke. She began to cry. The next morning Vincenzo spoke to her father.

There are boys at the fountain now, talking. Nonna looks up from the sidewalk, from the crack at which she was staring. The girls sit like bananas, all in a bunch. One of the boys flexes his arm muscles, like a real *malandrino.* The girls gaze at him, laughing. Nonna recognizes Lucia. She wears a tight pink top and short pants.

Why doesn't she hear Lucia's radio? Nonna wonders. A voice inside her head answers her question. Because the girl is with the boys. And when you are with them, Nonna says out loud, you do not need the radio.

The girls and boys look up. Nonna knows she must avoid them. They heard me, she whispers to herself, and now they will throw apples at me. *Santa Maria, madre di Dio.* She feels awkward as her feet strike the pavement. From behind she hears them calling.

Nonna! Who were you talking to? Hey, Nonna!

Nonna begins to run, and as she does her heavy purse bangs her side, up and down, again and again. Then the sound of their laughter fades away, and Nonna slows, feeling the banging inside her chest. They heard me, she thinks, and now they know my sin and will tell everyone. And then everyone, even the oldest parish priest, will know. I'll have to move to another neighborhood, she tells a fire hydrant. I'll pack my pans and the Madonnina and flee. Yet I have done that already two times. First from New Jersey, then when I was punished by the machines who flattened my house down. The woman doesn't count the move from Naples, when her family fled *miseria* and the coming war, nor the move from her parents' house when she married Vincenzo.

He would not have wanted her to be so lonely, she thinks. She is lucid, then again confused. Vincenzo understood why she could bear no children; it was because of their sin. Perhaps now that everybody knows, she thinks, she will not have to move any more. Maybe since the whole world knows, I can finally rest where I am now and be finished with my punishment. And then I'll die, Nonna says. And then if I have been punished enough I will be once again with my Vincenzo.

Her legs turn the corner for her. They are familiar with the streets. Nonna is on Flournoy, across from the church of Our Lady of Pompeii. At first the building looks strange to her, as if she were dreaming. The heavy wooden doors hang before her inside a gold-edged cloud. Nonna walks into the cloud. It is the blood in her head, the bone and the brain, she thinks. She pictures the fat butcher. The church's stone steps are hollowed, like spoons. Again she feels hungry. As she walks into the sunlight she wonders why she is wearing such a heavy coat. Nonna asks the doors her question. The doors stand high before her, silent. She pulls on their metal handles. The doors are locked.

She could go to the rectory and ask the priest for the keys. But they never give them to me, Nonna tells the doors. The priests tell me to come back for the Mass that evening, and I ask them if they don't think the saints and the Madonna are lonely with no one praying to them in the afternoons, and they say there are people all over the world who are praying, every moment of the day, but I don't believe them. If that was true it would be a different world, don't you think? She presses her cheek against the wood. Don't you think the world would be a little better? she says. Don't you understand me?

She hears something behind her and she turns. A dog. Panting before the first of the stone steps. Its ears are cocked. It is listening. Nonna laughs. The dog gives her a bark, and then from the middle of the park across the street comes the sound of a boy calling. He jumps in the sun, waving a dark stick. Nonna points to him. The boy is dark like the stick. A Mexican. So it is a Mexican dog, Nonna thinks. I would tell you that boy wants you, she tells the dog, but I don't know Mexican, and if I spoke to you in my tongue from Napoli you would just be confused. The dog turns and runs, as if understanding. Nonna laughs. What is she doing at the top of the church steps? She knows the church is locked during the afternoons because of the vandals. Haven't the priests so often told her that?

Her hand grasps the iron railing. She must be careful because of her legs. They get too tired from all the time holding her up. When she reaches the sidewalk she stops and faces the church and kneels, making the sign of the cross. Then she walks again down Flournoy Street.

Why was I at the church? she thinks. She makes the sign of the cross and smiles as she walks past the rectory, and now she remembers the church-basement meeting she attended because of the paper she had signed. It is good to sit with *paesani*, she thinks, and she pictures the faces of the neighborhood people, then the resolute eyes and mouth of the woman who gave the big speech.

How much intelligence the woman has! Nonna notices that her hands are moving together, clapping. It is good to clap, good for the blood, like eating the cloves of *aglio*. She stops clapping. But only in the meetings. The woman had said once and for all that it was the mayor's fault.

Vincenzo, Nonna whispers. She sees his still face, sleeping on a soft pillow. His mouth is turned down into a frown. Vincenzo, I tell you, it was not your fault.

Nonna closes her eyes. She feels dizzy. It was the meeting, all the talk, the excitement, the smoke. Then she realizes that was years ago, but she feels she had just been talking with her Vincenzo. Had he been at the meeting? No. He died long before the neighborhood changed. Before the students came. The *stranieri*. Before the Mexicans crept into the holes left by the *compari*. Then she must be walking home from his funeral. It was held at Our Lady of Pompeii. No, someone drove her home from the cemetery in a long black car. Where is home? she thinks. Where am I walking to? She pictures the faces of her parents, the rooms in the house in Napoli, the house in New Jersey, Vincenzo's house, the house in Chicago, and the dust and the machines. Then—

Two rooms.

Nonna remembers where she lives now.

She worries that she has left something burning on the stove. Was it neck bones? Was that what she had taken out for her supper? Or was it meat in the white cartons? Had she bought brains? She cannot think. Her legs are very tired. She will eat, if it is time, when she gets home.

The color of the sky is changing, and the traffic grows more heavy in the streets. It must be time, Nonna says to herself. She wishes to hurry so she won't be late. She does not like to eat when it is dark out. When it is dark she prays, then goes to bed. That is why there is the night, so people have a time for that.

Nonna approaches the street corner, and when she sees a

woman coming out of Speranza's doorway with a bag of groceries she remembers that she is out shopping. So that is why she's worn her heavy coat! Of course! But first she took a walk. The afternoon had been very nice, very pleasant. Did she enjoy herself? she wonders. It is difficult to decide. Finally she thinks yes, but only if she can remember what she is outside shopping for. What is it? It was on the tip of her tongue. What was it that she needed?

She turns at the door, and as she opens it she realizes that this store is no longer the Speranza Bakery. It is the Mexican grocery. She is frightened. Her legs carry her forward, out of habit. A man behind the counter looks up at her and nods. Now that he's seen her she cannot turn around and leave, she thinks. She hopes the Mexican will not ask her what she wants. What would she say? Her feet move slowly down the first aisle. Her hands draw together the flaps of her coat.

Well, she thinks, I must need something. She does not want a can of vegetables, nor any of the juices in heavy bottles. She sees the butcher's case and tries to remember if she needs meat. Then she pictures neck bones in a pan atop her stove. She must hurry, she thinks, before they burn.

Cereal, vinegar, *biscotti* in paper boxes. Cottage cheese or eggs? Nonna's heart beats loudly when she sees a stack of red apples, but she remembers how difficult apples are to chew, and she is too impatient now to cut them first into tiny pieces. Nonna smiles. Vincenzo had always said she was a patient woman. But not any longer. Not with hard red apples and a sharp knife.

Then she sees the bananas and, excited, she remembers.

What she needs is next to the counter. In plastic bags. Nonna is so happy that tears come to her eyes. So this is why she was outside, she thinks, why she is now inside this strange store. She'd wanted to try the freckled Mexican flat breads.

Hadn't someone before been telling her about them? Nonna holds the package in her hands and thinks. She cannot remember, but she is sure it had been someone. The intelligent woman with the petition paper or maybe the sad girl in the bookstore who prayed for just one baby. Someone who explained that her punishment was nearly over, that soon she would be with her Vincenzo. That these were the breads that were too simple to have been baked with yeast, that these did not rise, round and golden, like other breads, like women fortunate enough to feel their bellies swell, their breasts grow heavy with the promise of milk, but instead these stayed in one shape, simple, flat.

The dark man behind the counter nods and smiles.

Perhaps, Nonna thinks as her fingers unclasp her heavy purse and search for the coins her eyes no longer clearly see, perhaps bread is just as good this way.

# The Eyes of Children

The two seventh-grade girls came running to the playground, their pink cheeks streaked with tears, the pleated skirts of their navy-blue uniform skirts snapping in the wind. It was a windy Friday. Some of the children looked up at the sky to see if it would rain. They gathered in loose bunches by the gate near Sister Immaculata, the sixth-grade teacher, her skirts swirling like a child's pennant caught in a stiff breeze. The black folds of her habit whipped away behind her, flapping toward the gate and the alleyway, now shifting as the wind shifted, as she turned to face the wind. Dry leaves and scraps of paper whirled in circles on the ground beneath the basketball hoops. Dust stung the children's eyes. Not even Patrick Riley, the tallest eighth grader and captain of the basketball team, risked trying a shot against the wind. He sat on the parish basketball against the fence, flanked by his teammates, who chewed their fingernails or stood, hands in pockets, turning into the wind like Sister Immaculata.

Gino Martini, a dark seventh grader, knew he would have tried a shot. He stood near the players, fighting a yawn, his skinny arms folded across his chest. If he had the ball, he'd put it up. The ball would fall cleanly through the chain net, and everyone would cheer him.

A yellowed sheet of newspaper rose suddenly in the air and slammed into the playground fence, spreading flat against the weave of chain link. Gino was sleepy from serving the week's 6:45 morning Masses. He stared at a light-haired girl whose name he didn't know, watching how the wind pressed her skirt back against her legs. The blonde girl was pretty and stood all by herself, but Gino was shy and she was an eighth grader. The only seventh-grade boys the eighth-grade girls talked to were the guys on the school team. Gino had wanted to be on the team, but his father insisted he work after school, to learn responsibility, the value of a dollar. His mother insisted he serve God by being an altar boy. He had to obey. So no one knew him. The pretty girl didn't look at him, and Mrs. Bagnola and Sister Bernadette walked past her toward Sister Immaculata, and Mrs. Bagnola looked at her wristwatch and shook her head. The wind blew. Traffic rushed by in the street. Someday, Gino thought, I'll be part of something wonderful someday. Then everyone heard the cries of the two girls who ran inside the fence bordering the playground, and the girls grabbed the arms of their teachers, and the children crowded around them, pushed by the wind.

"The church!" shouted Donna Pietro, sobbing against Bernadette's chest.

"He was there," Maureen Ostrowski screamed, "he was there, in the church!" Her hands squeezed Mrs. Bagnola's arm.

"There now," Bernadette said. She stroked Donna's dark hair. "Take deep breaths. You've frightened yourselves."

"We—" Donna cried. "We didn't do anything, Sister!"

"All of a sudden he was just there!" Maureen said. "And he was bleeding!"

"Who?" Mrs. Bagnola said. Her hands grasped Maureen's shoulders and shook them until the girl's eyes steadied.

"Start from the beginning," Sister Immaculata said.

Donna gulped a breath, then stared at the sky. "Maureen forgot her scarf, Sister, so after lunch we went to church."

"During choir practice, Sister," Maureen said. "This morning."

"Maureen left her scarf up in the loft during choir practice," Donna said.

"It was my mother's." Maureen stomped her foot. "And she didn't know I borrowed it." The girl began to cry.

"So you two went to the choir loft," Mrs. Bagnola prodded.

"We should send someone to the rectory," Immaculata said.

"Not yet," Bernadette said. She looked at Mrs. Bagnola, then at the two girls. "You went up to the loft?"

"We didn't do anything, Sister!" Donna said. "Then all of a sudden he was there." She spread her arms and bent at the waist. "At the top of the loft by the stairs, just looking at us!" Donna again began to cry.

"Who?" Bernadette said.

"We thought he was Mr. Lindsey," Maureen said in a low voice. She wiped her tears with her fingertips. Mr. Lindsey was the parish choirmaster. "But he didn't say anything when we said hello—"

"We said, 'Good afternoon, Mr. Lindsey,'" Donna said. "We only whispered."

"—and then he turned, and his face was horrible and bleeding." Maureen's lips quivered. She stared out at the street. "And he wouldn't move or anything. He just stood there, blood dripping from his face. We couldn't run because he was by the stairs. Donna screamed—"

"We both screamed, Sister," Donna said.

"—and then he wasn't there anymore, and then we heard someone making noise downstairs in the church."

"Send a boy to the rectory," Bernadette told Mrs. Bagnola.

Gino waved his hand and bounced on his toes. Since he served so many Masses, it was only fair that he be picked. But Mrs. Bagnola's eyes looked beyond him over the crush of children. She motioned to Patrick Riley.

"—down the steps," Maureen was saying. She held out one hand as if she were grasping a railing. "And there were drops of blood on the marble—"

"Tiny drops of blood," Donna said. She hugged herself and shook.

"—didn't step in them, Sister, because we were afraid! He was horrible, standing there by the stairs holding the door open like he wanted us to come to him. And behind him was the big stained-glass window." Maureen made the sign of the cross. Around Gino some of the children crossed themselves too.

"I didn't want to get any of the blood on my shoes," Donna said. "These are my only pair of good shoes!"

"It's all right, Donna," Sister Bernadette said. "Your shoes are fine."

"And in the window Jesus was looking down on us, pointing to his Sacred Heart. And all we could see then was that big window. All the colors. The bright light." Maureen looked into the distance.

"I'll throw them away," Donna said, lifting her feet. "Even if the blood just got on the bottom! I'll throw them in a furnace! They'll burn, won't they, Sister?"

"We'll clean your shoes in Mother Superior's office," Bernadette said.

Mrs. Bagnola stepped forward. "This man, he didn't say anything to you or do anything, did he?"

The girls didn't move, then stared at each other and shook their heads.

"Thank God," said Sister Bernadette.

Her words rippled through the children. Some girls nodded and grabbed one another's hands. Donna ground the bottoms of her shoes on the asphalt. Maureen held one arm at her side, her finger pointing to her heart. Mrs. Bagnola checked her watch and nodded to Immaculata and Bernadette, and Bernadette blew her whistle, and the children assembled in three lines that buzzed with talk. Sister Bernadette left the playground first, walking between Maureen and Donna, shrinking as she moved up the alley that led to the school. Already the little children were marching toward school from their smaller playground behind the gymnasium across the street. The children sang a merry song as they marched. Gino watched everything, standing silently in line, thinking maybe there had been a terrible car crash and the man had smashed his face against the windshield, then run to the church looking for a priest who'd give him the Last Rites. Gino wished Mrs. Bagnola had chosen him to go to the rectory. He wanted to see the drops of blood, and if they made a trail, and where the trail led. If the priest followed the trail, they'd find the man and could hear his confession. A girl in the front of Gino's line began to cry. Maybe she got a cinder in her eye, Gino thought. Sister Immaculata's group walked from the playground. The wind was blowing up lots of dust. The man was most likely waiting inside one of the confessionals, and right now Father Manning was probably forgiving all his sins. The girl wept, circled now by other girls. It wasn't a big deal. Just a man and some blood. A stray mutt ran past the children nearest the fence. Mrs. Bagnola shooed the dog away, and the wind blew and bent the heads of the children, and Gino's line began the march up the alley to the school.

*    *    *

The afternoon passed slowly. All the seventh graders stared at the fifth row, at the pair of empty desks. Mother Superior explained that Donna and Maureen had been given the afternoon off. Hands rose in the air. Mother Superior said there would be no discussion, and when she knelt next to the wooden platform beneath Sister Bernadette's desk and took out her rosary Gino realized they'd spend the afternoon praying. The children knelt, as noisily as falling blocks, on the wooden floor. When Sister Bernadette returned to the classroom Gino tried to read her face, but the woman was as somber and unreadable as Latin. Gino's class then prayed three rosaries: one for Maureen, one for Donna, the third for the bleeding man.

"It's an unfortunate incident," Bernadette told the class. She stared at the clock on the wall. There were a few minutes before the bell.

"The church has always been a refuge for the sick and needy," Sister continued. "The doors of the parish are always open. The priests receive calls at all hours of the day and night. Once, at midnight, a poor woman knocked on the rectory door because she had no food to feed her hungry children and she was tempted to go out and steal, and the priests gave her food. Another time a very rich man was driving around in his limousine thinking of committing the unforgivable sin of suicide, because you know that wealth does not bring a person peace or true happiness, and the priests listened to him and gave him their blessing, and the rich man renounced all his earthly belongings and went on to live a life dedicated to Christ." She smiled. "So you see, children, sometimes the church does have unhappy visitors, but God greets them all with forgiveness and love." The final bell then sounded.

The sky looked like it would rain. Gino thought about Sister's words as he hurried home. Maybe, he thought, there hadn't been a car accident. Maybe the man was just an unhappy visitor. But then why was he bleeding?

Gino hoped it wouldn't rain until after he finished his paper route. As he walked past the playground he heard a bouncing basketball and saw Patrick Riley and his friends leaning against the basket nearest the street. The boys didn't answer Gino's shy hello. Gino walked slowly outside the fence so he could overhear what they said.

"—all over the Saint Joseph's side aisle," Patrick was saying. "Man, I couldn't believe it."

"Those girls were awful lucky," one boy said.

"Lucky?" another said. "Lucky ain't the word."

"Nobody knows what he would of done if he'd of caught them."

"He probably had a knife. Or a razor. Maybe a switchblade. He could have slit their throats."

"Nah."

"Sure. A strange guy bleeding all over the church? Whatdya think?"

"He sure wasn't there to make no stations of the cross!"

The boys laughed.

Patrick bounced the ball. "Father Pinky said he was some kind of lunatic. You know, out of his mind, not knowing what he was doing."

"Rita Binetti and her friends were talking about him maybe being a saint or something like that."

"I heard them. Felice Hernandez said maybe it was a vision. You know, like our Lady of Guadalupe, or Lourdes."

"Then how could he leave behind all that blood?"

"Visions can bleed."

"No."

"Yeah."

"Yeah, maybe the blood can cure you if you touch it."

"Nah," Patrick said. "He was a lunatic."

"He could have been a miracle, you know. He didn't hurt them. He had them trapped up in the choir loft. All they got was a little scared."

"Rita said maybe he was Jesus."

"What's she know? Her brother is so stupid he flunked second grade."

Gino crossed the street, thinking of the two girls. Donna scraping her shoes on the ground. Maureen holding one hand to her chest, like the window of the Sacred Heart. Maureen said that she remembered the window because of the bright light. But it was a cloudy day. Gino gazed at the sky. Maybe the man *was* Jesus, Gino considered. And Jesus knew in his infinite wisdom that Maureen would forget her mother's scarf, and the girls would search the loft for it, and then he'd appear to them, right beneath the stained-glass window so they'd know, and he'd leave behind the trail of his most sacred blood, and the trail would lead . . . Gino stared at the sidewalk. The trail of blood would lead to God the Father, of course. The boy walked quickly now, excited. Maureen and Donna were awfully lucky to have been chosen, Gino thought, but like in all the other visitation stories at first the people wouldn't believe them, and the priests and Church authorities would have to try to shake their faith. But in the end, after many miracles, everyone would believe them and the girls would be very holy, and after they died they'd be saints. Yes. Gino ran home now. He no longer cared if it rained. He wanted to hurry to the newspaper office to see if the news was on the front page. He'd believe in the miracle from the start, he decided. Yes, he would believe. No doubt. Already he believed.

*   *   *

His alarm clock woke him early the next morning. The sky behind his bedroom shade was dark. All his brothers and sisters were still sleeping, so Gino was quiet as he slipped his clothes off their hangers and then tiptoed to the bathroom to wash. He had time, he thought. He didn't need to rush. Usually the alarm would shriek for a full minute before he'd wake, but this morning he sat up in bed, aware, a moment or two before the first ring. He was careful not to swallow any toothpaste as he brushed his teeth. He didn't want to break his Communion fast. Especially today, the first day after the miracle. In the kitchen he glanced at the clock, always set ten minutes fast so everyone would be on time. He penciled a note and left it on the table, next to the day's bread. WENT TO SERVE. Slapping his pants pocket to make sure he had his house key, he grabbed his jacket. The front door clicked softly behind him.

Only a white milk truck idling in a cloud of exhaust was out on the street. Gino walked along the sidewalk darkened by the evening's rain. The night had seen a real storm. He stepped over flattened leaves, twigs, branches thick as his arms. There'd been plenty of lightning and low, rolling thunder, the kind that lasted several seconds and rattled the windowpanes and terrified Gino's younger brothers and sisters, but he hadn't been afraid. The storm was right, wonderful. Gino knew it had stormed because the girls had seen Jesus in the church.

The miracle hadn't been in the newspaper. Gino had wondered why, then figured that the people who printed the newspaper weren't Catholics. At supper when he told his parents about the vision, they misunderstood. No, he argued. No. You have to believe!

"Eat," his father had told him.

They'd see, Gino thought. And he would be special because he knew and believed from the beginning. He walked past the playground and then the grammar school, breathing the cool air that tasted wet and as dark as tree bark, and was still fresh from the night's furious storm, then cut through the empty parish courtyard and entered through the side doorway of the church.

The dark hallway leading to the altar boys' room stretched ahead of him. He dipped his fingers into the holy water fount and made the sign of the cross. On the wooden floor by the fount were pages torn from a parish hymnal. Gino picked the pages up, then saw the edge of another torn page crushed beneath the inner side door. What? He opened the inner door of the church.

His breath tripped in his throat. Covering the marble floor were scores of shattered vigil lights. The wrought-iron stand that had held the glass cups lay on its side. More hymnals lay flung to the floor. Gino looked at Mary's side altar. The blue embroidered cloth hanging across its marble front was slashed. All six gold candlesticks were knocked down, and each candle was broken. Flowers and more vigil lights lay smashed on the altar's steps. The heavy tabernacle beneath the statue of the Virgin was tipped from its base, as if shoved by a giant, and rested at a dizzy angle. Glass crunched beneath his feet as he stepped forward. The boy turned and ran.

Gino ran up the dark hallway to the altar boys' room. Pitch black. His fingers found the light switch. Nothing there had been damaged. No one else was there. He hurried down the length of the dark passageway that ran behind the center altar and led to the sacristy and rectory, calling out, "Father! Father!" But when he heard no response, he stopped in the darkness and listened to his pounding heart. There was nothing to do but return to the servers' room and dress for Mass.

Numb, he took his black cassock from the closet, then threw on the white surplice. Then he buttoned the top button of his white shirt. His fingers were shaking. Gino looked at his hands, then genuflected and held them for a moment to his face.

He took a long breath and walked again down the passageway, hearing the echo of his footsteps. This time someone was there— a priest, smoke curling from a cigarette.

"Father!" Gino cried. "Father, the church!"

"I know," Father Manning said, cinching the cord around his alb.

"But Father—"

The priest walked toward him and put a hand on the boy's shoulder. "You'll forgive me. I don't usually smoke here. I don't want to give you a bad example. You don't smoke, do you, Gino?"

"No, Father." The hand still gripped his shoulder.

"Good," the priest said. "I wish I shared your self-control." He withdrew his arm.

"But the church—" Gino began.

"We'll clean the mess up before too many people see it. Don't be upset."

"But I thought it was a miracle, Father."

"What?" Manning said.

Gino looked away, then back at the priest's face. "But I thought that Jesus—"

Manning snorted, then took a deep drag off his cigarette. "There was nothing miraculous about what happened here." Smoke streamed from his mouth in an angry hiss. "Believe me." He stubbed out his cigarette, then turned to finish dressing.

Gino nodded, confused, events still piecing themselves together. He walked to the small wine closet for the cruets. Manning called out, "Full," so Gino filled one of the cruets with wine, the other with cold water. The cold water splashed in the bowl of the sink. Gino set the cruets beside the dish and cloth and patens that rested on the small table next to the altar, then returned to the sacristy for the pole used to light the candles, and he lit the center pair—it was to be a low Mass—and tears welled in his eyes.

No miracle. A flush every bit as burning as the flame washed over him. Fool, he thought. To think he was special. To believe. For a moment he stood quietly at the altar, holding the flame up to the tall candle, feeling his tears drip from his cheeks down to the altar cloth.

Then a sudden sorrow fell over him. All at once the world seemed very dark and very big.

# My Mother's Stories

They were going to throw her away when she was a baby. The doctors said she was too tiny, too frail, that she wouldn't live. They performed the baptism right there in the sink between their pots of boiling water and their rows of shining instruments, chose who would be her godparents, used water straight from the tap. Her father, however, wouldn't hear one word of it. He didn't listen to their *she'll only die anyway* and *please give her to us* and *maybe we can experiment.* No, the child's father stood silently in the corner of the room, the back of one hand wiping his mouth and thick moustache, his blue eyes fixed on the black mud that caked his pants and boots.

*Nein*, he said, finally. *Nein*, die anyvay.

With this, my mother smiles. She enjoys imitating the man's thick accent. She enjoys the sounds, the images, the memory. Her brown eyes look past me into the past. She draws a quick breath, then continues.

You can well imagine the rest. How the farmer took his wife and poor sickly child back to his farm. How the child was nursed, coddled, fed cow's milk, straight from the tops of the buckets —the rich, frothy cream. How the child lived. If she hadn't, I wouldn't be here now in the corner of this room, my eyes fixed on her, my mother and her stories. For now the sounds and pictures are *my* sounds and pictures. Her memory, my memory.

I stand here, remembering. The family moved. To Chicago, the city by the Great Lake, the city of jobs, money, opportunity. Away from northwestern Ohio's flat fields. The child grew. She is a young girl now, enrolled in school, Saint Teresa's, virgin. Chicago's Near North Side. The 1930s. And she is out walking with her girlfriend, a dark Sicilian. Spring, late afternoon. My mother wears a small pink bow in her brown hair.

Then from across the black pavement of the school playground comes a lilting stream of foreign sound, language melodic, of the kind sung solemnly at High Mass. The Sicilian girl turns quickly, smiling. The voice is her older brother's, and he too is smiling as he stands inside the playground fence. My mother turns but does not smile. She is modest. Has been properly, strictly raised. Is the last of seven children and, therefore, the object of many scolding eyes and tongues. Her name is Mary.

Perhaps our Mary, being modest, is somewhat frightened. The boy behind the high fence is older than she, is in high school, is finely muscled, dark, deeply tanned. Around his neck hang golden things glistening on a thin chain. He wears a sleeveless shirt—his undershirt. Mary doesn't know whether to stay with her young friend or to continue walking. She stays, but she looks away from the boy's dark eyes and gazes instead at the worn belt around his thin waist.

That was my parents' first meeting. His name is Tony, as is mine. This is not a story she tells willingly, for she sees nothing special in it. All of the embellishments are mine. I've had to drag the story out of her, nag her from room to room. Ma? Ask your father, she tells me. I ask my father. He looks up from his newspaper, then starts to smile. He's in a playful mood. He laughs, then says: I met your mother in Heaven.

She, in the hallway, overhears. Bull, she says, looking again past me. He didn't even know I was alive. My father laughs behind his newspaper. I was Eva's friend, she says, and we were walking home from school . . . I watch him, listening as he lowers the paper to look at her. She tells the story.

She knows how to tell a pretty good story, I think. She's a natural. She knows how to use her voice, when to pause, how to pace, what expressions to mask her face with. Her hand slices out the high fence. She's not in the same room with you when she really gets at it; her stories take her elsewhere, somewhere back. She's there again, back on a 1937 North Side side street. My father and I are only witnesses.

Picture her, then. A young girl, frightened, though of course for no good reason—my father wouldn't have harmed her. I'll vouch for him. I'm his first son. But she didn't know that as the afternoon light turned low and golden from between distant buildings. Later she'd think him strange and rather arrogant, flexing his tanned muscles before her inside the fence, like a bull before a heifer. And for years (wasted ones, I think) she didn't give him a second thought, or so she claims—the years that she dated boys who were closer to her kind. These are her words.

Imagine those years, years of *ja Fraülein, ja, bitte, entschuldigen Sie,* years of pale Johnnys and freckled Fritzes and hairy Hermans, towheads all, who take pretty Mary dancing and roller-skating and sometimes downtown on the El to the movie theaters on State Street to see Clark Gable, and who buy popcorn and ice cream for her and, later, cups of coffee which she then drank with cream, and who hold her small hand and look up at the Chicago sky as they walk with her along the dark city streets to her father's flat on Fremont. Not *one* second thought? I cannot believe it. And whenever I interrupt to ask, she waves me away like I'm an insect flying between her eyes and what she really sees. I fold my arms, but I listen.

She was sweeping. This story always begins with that detail. With broom in hand. Nineteen years old and employed as a milliner and home one Saturday and she was sweeping. By then both her parents were old. Her mother had grown round, ripe like a fruit, like she would. Her father now fashioned things out of wood. A mound of fluff and sawdust grows in the center of the room and she is humming, perhaps something from Glenn Miller, or she might have sung, as I've heard her do while ironing on the back porch, when from behind the locked back screen door there was suddenly a knock and it was my father, smiling.

She never tells the rest of the details. But this was the afternoon he proposed. Why he chose that afternoon, or even afternoon at all, are secrets not known to me. I ask her and she evades me. *Ask your father.* I ask him and he says he doesn't know. Then he looks at her and laughs, his eyes smiling, and I can see that he is making up some lie to tell me. I watch her. Because I loved her so much I couldn't wait until that night, he says. My mother laughs and shakes her head. No, he says, I'll tell you the truth this time. Now you really know he's lying. I was just walking down the street and the idea came to me. See, it was awful hot. His hand on his forehead, he pretends he had sunstroke. My mother laughs less.

There were problems. Another of her stories. They follow one after the next like cars out on the street—memories, there is just no stopping them. Their marriage would be mixed. Not in the religious sense—that would have been unthinkable—but in terms of language, origin, tradition. Like mixing your clubs with your hearts, mixing this girl from Alsace and Liechtenstein with this boy from Sicily. Her family thought she was, perhaps, lowering herself. An Italian? Why not your kind? And his family, likewise, felt that he would be less than happy with a non-Sicilian girl. She's so skinny, they told him. *Misca!* Mary's skin and bones. When she has the first baby she'll bleed to death. And what will she feed you? Cabbages? *Marry your own kind.*

At their Mass someone failed to play "Ave Maria." Since that was the cue for my mother to stand and then to place a bouquet of flowers on Mary's side altar, she remained at the center altar, still kneeling, waiting patiently for the organist to begin. He was playing some other song, not "Ave Maria." The priest gestured to her. My mother shook her head.

She was a beautiful bride, and she wore a velvet dress. You should see the wedding photograph that hangs in the hallway of their house in Chicago. Imagine a slender brown-haired bride in white velvet shaking her head at the priest who'd just married her. No, the time is not yet for the young woman to stand, for her to kneel in prayer before the altar of the Virgin. This is her wedding day, remember. She is waiting for "Ave Maria."

She is waiting to this day, for the organist never did play the song, and the priest again motioned to her, then bent and whispered in her ear, and then, indignant, crushed, the young bride finally stood and angrily, solemnly, sadly waited for her maid of honor to gather the long train of her flowing velvet dress, and together the two marched to the Virgin's side altar.

She tells this story frequently, whenever there is a wedding. I think that each time she begins the story she is tempted to change the outcome, to make the stupid organist suddenly stop and slap his head. To make the organist begin the chords of "Ave Maria." That kind of power isn't possible in life. The organist didn't stop or slap his head.

I wonder if the best man tipped him. If my father was angry enough to complain. If the muscles in his jaws tightened, if his hands turned to fists, if anyone waited for the organist out in the parking lot. I am carried away.

Details *are* significant. Literally they can be matters of life and death. An organist makes an innocent mistake in 1946 and for the rest of her life a woman is compelled to repeat a story, as if for her the moment has not yet been fixed, as if by remembering and then speaking she could still influence the pattern of events since passed.

*   *   *

Life and death . . .

I was hoping the counterpart wouldn't be able to work its way into this story. But it's difficult to keep death out. The final detail. Always coming along unexpectedly, the uninvited guest at the banquet, acting as if you were supposed to have known all along that he'd get there, expecting to be seated and for you to offer him a drink.

My father called yesterday. He said he was just leaving work to take my mother to the hospital again. Tests. I shouldn't call her yet. No need to alarm her, my father said. Just tests. We'll keep you posted. My mother is in the hospital. I am not Meursault.

I must describe the counterpart, return, begin again. With 1947, with my mother, delirious, in labor. Brought to the hospital by my father early on a Saturday, and on Monday laboring still. The doctors didn't believe in using drugs. She lay three days, terrified, sweating. On Monday morning they brought my father into the room, clad in an antiseptic gown, his face covered by a mask. She mistook him for one of the doctors. When he bent to kiss her cheek she grabbed his arm and begged him. Doctor, doctor, can you give me something for the pain?

That Monday was Labor Day. Ironies exist. Each September now, on my older sister Diana's birthday, my mother smiles and tells that story.

Each of us was a difficult birth. Did my father's family know something after all? The fourth, my brother Bob, nearly killed her. He was big, over ten pounds. The doctors boasted, proudly, that Bob set their personal record. The fifth child, Jim, weighed almost ten-and-a-half pounds, and after Jim the doctors fixed my mother so that there wouldn't be a sixth child. I dislike the word *fixed*, but it's an appropriate word, I think.

When I was a child my mother once took Diana and me shopping, to one of those mom-and-pop stores in the middle of the block. I remember a blind man who always sat on a wooden milk crate outside the store with his large dog. I was afraid of the dog. Inside the store we shopped, and my mother told us stories, and the three of us were laughing. She lifted a carton of soda as she spoke. Then the rotted cardboard bottom of the carton gave way and the soda bottles fell. The bottles burst. The sharp glass bounced. She shouted and we screamed, and as she tells this story she makes a point of remembering how worried she was that the glass had reached our eyes. But then some woman in the store told her she was bleeding. My mother looked down. Her foot was cut so badly that blood gushed from her shoe. I remember the picture, but then the face of the blind man's dog covers up the image and I see the wooden milk crate, the scratched white cane.

The middle child, Linda, is the special one. It was on a Christmas morning when they first feared she was deaf. Either Diana or I knocked over a pile of toy pans and dishes — a pretend kitchen — directly behind the one-year-old child playing on the floor, and Linda, bright and beautiful, did not move. She played innocently, unaffected, removed from the sound that had come to life behind her. Frantic, my mother then banged two of the metal dinner plates behind Linda's head. Linda continued playing, in a world by herself, softly cooing.

What I can imagine now from my mother's stories is a long procession of doctors, specialists, long trips on the bus. Snow-covered streets. Waiting in sterile waiting rooms. Questions. Answers. More questions. Tests. Hope. Then, no hope. Then guilt came. Tony and Mary blamed themselves.

Forgive the generalities. She is a friendly woman; she likes to make others laugh. Big-hearted, perhaps to a fault, my mother has a compulsion to please. I suspect she learned that trait as a child, being the youngest of so many children. Her parents were quite old, and as I piece her life together I imagine them strict, resolute, humorless. My mother would disagree were she to hear me. But I suspect that she's been bullied and made to feel inferior, by whom or what I don't exactly know, and now to compensate, she works very hard at pleasing.

She tells a story about how she would wash and wax her oldest brother's car and how he'd pay her one penny. How each day, regardless of the weather, she'd walk to a distant newsstand and buy for her father the *Abendpost*. How she'd be sent on especially scorching summer days by another of her brothers for an ice cream cone, and how as she would gingerly carry it home she'd take not one lick. How could she resist? In my mother's stories she's always the one who's pleasing.

Her brown eyes light up, and like a young girl she laughs. She says she used to cheat sometimes and take a lick. Then, if her brother complained, she'd claim the ice cream had been melted by the sun. Delighted with herself, she smiles. Her eyes again twinkle with light.

I am carried away again. If it were me in that story I'd throw the cone to the ground and tell my brother to get his own damn ice cream.

*    *    *

You've seen her. You're familiar with the kind of house she lives in, the red brick two-flat. You've walked the tree-lined city street. She hangs the family's wash up in the small backyard, the next clothespin in her mouth. She picks up the squashed paper cups and the mustard-stained foot-long hot dog wrappers out in the front that the kids from the public school leave behind as they walk back from the Tastee-Freeze on the corner. During the winter she sweeps the snow. Wearing a discarded pair of my father's earmuffs. During the fall she sweeps leaves. She gets angry when the kids cut through the backyard, leaving the chain-link gates open, for the dog barks then and the barking bothers her. The dog, a female schnauzer mutt, is called Alfie. No ferocious beast—the plastic BEWARE OF DOG signs on the gates have the harsher bite. My mother doesn't like it when the kids leave the alley gate open. She talks to both her neighbors across both her fences. Wearing one of Bob's old sweaters, green and torn at the elbow, she bends to pick up a fallen autumn twig. She stretches to hang the wash up—the rows of whites, then the coloreds. She lets Alfie out and checks the alley gate.

Summer visit. Over a mug of morning coffee I sit in the kitchen reading the *Sun-Times.* Alfie in the backyard barks and barks. My mother goes outside to quiet her. I turn the page, reading of rape or robbery, something distant. Then I hear the dog growl, then again bark. I go outside.

My mother is returning to the house, her face red, angry. Son of a B, she says. I just caught some punk standing outside the alley gate teasing Alfie. She points. He was daring her to jump at him, and the damn kid was holding one of the garbage can lids over his head, just waiting to hit her. My mother demonstrates with her hands.

I run to the alley, ready to fight, to defend. But there is no one in the alley.

My mother stands there on the narrow strip of sidewalk, her hands now at her sides. She looks tired. Behind her in the yard is an old table covered with potted plants. Coleus, philodendron, wandering Jew. One of the planters, a statue of the Sacred Heart of Jesus. Another, Mary with her white ceramic hands folded in prayer. Mother's Day presents of years ago. Standing in the bright morning sun.

And when I came out, my mother continues, the punk just looked at me, real snotty-like, like he was *daring* me, and then he said come on and hit me, lady, you just come right on and hit me. I'll show you, lady, come on. And then he used the *F* word. She shakes her head and looks at me.

Later, inside, as she irons one of my father's shirts, she tells me another story. It happened last week, at night. The ten o'clock news was on. Time to walk Alfie. She'd been feeling lousy all day so Jim took the dog out front instead.

So he was standing out there waiting for Alfie to finish up her business when all of a sudden he hears this engine and he looks up, and you know what it was, Tony? Can you guess, of all things? It was this car, this *car*, driving right down along the sidewalk with its lights out. Jim said he dove straight for the curb, pulling poor Alfie in the middle of number two right with him. And when they went past him they swore at him and threw an empty beer can at him. She laughs and looks at me, then stops ironing and sips her coffee. Her laughter is from fear. Well, you should have heard your little brother when he came back in. Boy, was he steaming! They could have killed him they were driving so fast. The cops caught the kids up at Tastee-Freeze corner. We saw the squad car lights from the front windows. It was a good thing Jim took the dog out that night instead of me. She sprinkles the shirt with water from a Pepsi bottle. Can you picture your old mother diving then for the curb?

She makes a tugging gesture with her hands. Pulling the leash. Saving herself and Alfie. Again she laughs. She tells the story again when Jim comes home.

*　　*　　*

At first the doctors thought she had disseminated lupus erythematosus. *Lupus* means wolf. It is primarily a disease of the skin. As lupus advances, the victim's face becomes ulcerated by what are called butterfly eruptions. The face comes to resemble a wolf's. Disseminated lupus attacks the joints as well as the internal organs. There isn't a known cure.

And at first they made her hang. My mother. They made her buy a sling into which she placed her head, five times each day. Pulling her head from the other side was a heavy water bag. My father put the equipment up on the door of my bedroom. For years when I went to sleep I stared at that water bag. She had to hang for two-and-a-half hours each day. Those were the years that she read every book she could get her hands on.

And those were the years that she received the weekly shots, the cortisone, the steroids, that made her puff up, made her put on the weight the doctors are now telling her to get rid of.

Then one of the doctors died, and then she had to find new doctors, and then again she had to undergo their battery of tests. These new doctors told her that she probably didn't have lupus, that instead they thought she had severe rheumatoid arthritis, that the ten years of traction and corticosteroids had been a mistake. They gave her a drugstore full of pills then. They told her to lose weight, to exercise each night.

A small blackboard hangs over the kitchen sink. The markings put there each day appear to be Chinese. Long lines for these pills, dots for those, the letter *A* for yet another. A squiggly line for something else.

The new doctors taught her the system. When you take over thirty pills a day you can't rely on memory.

* * *

My father called again. He said there was nothing new. Mary is in the hospital again, and she's been joking that she's somewhat of a celebrity. So many doctors come in each day to see her. Interns. Residents. They hold conferences around her bed. They smile and read her chart. They question her. They thump her abdomen. They move her joints. They point. One intern asked her when she had her last menstrual cycle. My mother looked at the young man, then smiled and said twenty-some years ago but I couldn't for the life of me tell you which month. The intern's face quickly reddened. My mother's hysterectomy is written there in plain view on her chart.

They ask her questions and she recites her history like a litany.

Were the Ohio doctors right? Were they prophets? *Please give her to us. Maybe we can experiment.*

* * *

My father and I walk along the street. We've just eaten, then gone to Osco for the evening paper—an excuse, really, just to take a walk. And he is next to me suddenly bringing up the subject of my mother's health, just as suddenly as the wind from the lake shakes the thin branches of the trees. The moment is serious, I realize. My father is not a man given to unnecessary talk.

I don't know what I'd do without her, he says. I say nothing, for I can think of nothing to say. We've been together for over thirty years, he says. He pauses. For nearly thirty-four years. Thirty-four years this October. And, you know, you wouldn't think it, but I love her so much more now. He hesitates, and I look at him. He shakes his head and smiles. You know what I mean? he says. I say yes and we walk for a while in silence, and I think of what it must be like to live with someone for thirty-four years, but I cannot imagine it, and then I hear my father begin to talk about that afternoon's ball game—he describes at length and in comic detail a misjudged fly ball lost in apathy or ineptitude or simply in the sun—and for the rest of our walk home we discuss what's right and wrong with our favorite baseball team, our thorn-in-the-side Chicago Cubs.

*      *      *

I stand here, not used to speaking about things that are so close to me. I am used to veiling things in my stories, to making things wear masks, to telling my stories through masks. But my mother tells her stories openly, as she has done so all of her life—since she lived on her father's farm in Ohio, as she walked along the crowded 1930 Chicago streets, to my father overseas in her letters, to the five of us children, as we sat on her lap, as we played in the next room while she tended to our supper in the kitchen. She tells her stories to everyone, to anyone who will listen. She taught Linda to read her lips.

I learn now to read her lips.

*      *      *

And I imagine one last story.

Diana and I are children. Our mother is still young. Diana and I are outside on the sidewalk playing and it's summer. And we are young and full of play and happy, and we see a dog, and it comes toward us on the street. My sister takes my hand. She senses something, I think. The dog weaves from side to side. It's sick, I think. Some kind of lather is on its mouth. The dog growls. I feel Diana's hand shake.

Now we are inside the house, safe, telling our mother. Linda, Bob, and Jim are there. We are all the same age, all children. Our mother looks outside, then walks to the telephone. She returns to the front windows. We try to look out the windows too, but she pushes the five of us away.

No, she says. I don't want any of you to see this.

We watch her watching. Then we hear the siren of a police car. We watch our mother make the sign of the cross. Then we hear a shot. Another. I look at my sisters and brothers. They are crying. Worried, frightened, I begin to cry too.

Did it come near you? our mother asks us. Did it touch you? Any of you? Linda reads her lips. She means the funny dog. Or does she mean the speeding automobile with its lights off? The Ohio doctors? The boy behind the alley gate? The shards of broken glass? The wolf surrounded by butterflies? The ten-and-a-half pound baby?

Diana, the oldest, speaks for us. She says that it did not.

Our mother smiles. She sits with us. Then our father is with us. Bob cracks a smile, and everybody laughs. Alfie gives a bark. The seven of us sit closely on the sofa. Safe.

That actually happened, but not exactly in the way that I described it. I've heard my mother tell that story from time to time, at times when she's most uneasy, but she has never said what it was that she saw from the front windows. A good storyteller, she leaves what she has all too clearly seen to our imaginations.

I stand in the corner of this room, thinking of her lying now in the hospital.

\* \* \*

I pray none of us looks at that animal's face.

# *Ritual*

They sat in the boat, the two, the son and the father, but neither man knew what to say. It was summer. July. Above them the northern Wisconsin sky was blue and cloudless, so blue and cloudless that the tall stands of birch and pine on the shore seemed dwarfed, miniature; and the two men from the city felt that way themselves.

The son sat bare-chested in the front of the boat, an unlit cigarette between his teeth, casting. After his lure hit the water he counted one-one, two-two. Then he changed the rod to his other hand and began reeling in, firmly, silently, occasionally jerking the tip of his rod to one side or the other, to add to the movement of his lure, sometimes varying his speed, cranking the reel slowly at first and then more quickly, forcing the lure to act how he imagined a frog or a minnow might act: irrational, innocent, darting fearfully through the blue water toward the safety of the dark shadow of the boat. Each time the son cast, his lure returned empty, its spinning silver spoon shining brilliantly in the water. Then it would break the still surface of the lake, six, seven feet from the boat, and the son would stare at it and at the empty, still water behind it, and then he'd reel it slowly the rest of the way in.

The father's method was different. He stood quietly in the back of the small boat. Casting over his right shoulder, away from his son, the father waited until his lure struck the water and then he counted, one-two-three, four-five-six, and then he added a seven for good measure. Then, like the son, the man would change hands, and as he began reeling in he'd squat slowly down upon his faded green life preserver, usually bringing his hand up to check the blue Cubs cap on his head. He reeled steadily, the father, as evenly and methodically as he was able, and when his lure broke surface he continued to reel but then he'd raise his hands up to the level of his chest. Finally, when the lure was a foot or two away from the shadow of the boat, the father again stood and pointed the tip of his blunt rod toward the water, and with the lure he made two even figure eights. Then he'd pause, check his cap, and cast again.

Between the men was an empty seat. On the boat's curved bottom rested their two tackle boxes, a spare life preserver cushion, the net, a red thermos jug of water, the son's pack of cigarettes, the father's sandals. Next to the father was the gasoline tank. The lines running from it to the motor were tied beneath his seat. Beneath the son's seat was a rusted two-pound coffee can filled with cement. Their anchor, it was dry. It was tied with knotted clothesline to the front tip of the boat. Strands of dried milfoil clung to the gray rope. The two were allowing their small boat to drift.

Each casting toward the shoreline, toward the shadows beneath the trees, where the best fish might be hiding. The boat drifted parallel to the shore. Casting, then again casting. High above them in the sky flew a heron.

\*   \*   \*

*The heron flies high above them. Stately head drawn back, the easy wing flap, flight, gliding, the long legs trailing, over the small boat drifting parallel to the shoreline; the reach of wings, the effortless flap; the majestic head turns; the yellow eyes scan.*

*Fields of darkness and brightness. The bend at the point where the water grows more shallow; concentrated darkness, round blotches, irregular, rocks; and again the reach, the flap; between the rocks bright splashing, the water now glistening as it breaks in clean bright beads across the back of surfacing mallards. Wings stretch and beat, deep. Ease. Now over a white framework, its slanting edge lined with black semicircles. Adjacent, the shape of boat. The floor of the lake, a light rectangle; the prone forms of three animals, swimming; light reflecting, water splashing;*

around their legs and arms bright luminous concentric arcs. Gliding toward, suddenly, a glint in the now-dark field below; toward
the silver flash of fish, adrift, dead; and circling, spiraling, great
blue wings outstretched and dropping, gliding down to discover
the dead fish a thing not fish, a thing of wood or metal, not fish;
then turning and pushing behind the air beneath the two great
flapping pushing wings; the clap, clap, clap of great blue flapping,
flying, back over the light rectangle, the three swimmers, the row
of black circles edging the white dock, the pointed shape of boat,
and then around the shallow rocky point and then again over
the two heads, over and now beyond the shape of a small boat
drifting.
                              *   *   *

"You shouldn't stand," the son said.

He turned back toward the shore and watched the white curve
of his line fly nearly to the shadows and then fall, gracelessly, the
lure plopping without design or elegance to the lake's clear shal-
lows. The shadow of the heron overhead intersected his white
line. He counted one-one, two-two. Imagining a good fish lurking
near the approaching point between the rocks hearing the plop,
or at least sensing the plop, feeling its vibrations, the son reeled
in his line and willed the good fish to swim out from its hiding
place. Come on, he thought. The lure twirled in a jagged line back
toward the shadow of the boat. A fish could strike on any cast,
the son told himself. If not this cast, the next. The thing was to
be ready. The son felt he was ready as he looked over his right
shoulder at the man sitting in the rear of the boat, his hand up,
checking his baseball cap, now dropping the hand, now steadily
and immutably reeling.

"What?" his father said, not turning.

"You shouldn't stand," said the son. "You cast a shadow." His
lure was five feet now from the boat. It broke surface. There was
not a fish or even a turtle or a dragonfly following it. He turned
his head again to look up at the sun.

"The sun is almost behind us," he said, reeling in his line, "and when you stand you cast a shadow and the fish see the shadow and then don't bite."

It was logical. He was glad he was in the front of the boat. And he was glad he knew more about fishing than his father. The son shifted the unlit cigarette between his teeth. Drifting by the point now, he noticed a group of brown ducks squatting near the rocky shoreline, and around the rocks he saw the green skirts of algae rising and falling as the water gently lapped the rocks. Was it algae? He thought of hula dancers. Hula skirts. No good fish hiding near the rocks, he thought. The water there was too warm, too clear, too shallow.

His father hadn't answered him. The son let his comment ride, looking at the ducks, happy that he was in the front casting toward the left, ahead of the drifting boat and its shadows. A fish that struck from the front wouldn't be forewarned or frightened off. He then had the advantage. He looked back at his father.

"What fish?" his father finally said. He smiled, stood, cast.

The son shook his head. It was just like his father to be so pessimistic. The young man cast toward the ducks. The spoon on his lure tangled itself with his line, and his reel spun too quickly—the weight of the lure failed to evenly pull the ready spinning line—and in an attempt to stop it the son thumbed the reel and reeled in, but the line bunched up anyway, snarled. He stared at it and sighed. His lure sank beyond his sight in the water. Once again the son began to crank, but the line remained knotted in the face of the open reel, so he bit his cigarette and tugged one of the tangled loops of the line. That only knotted the line more tightly. Looking back at his father he placed his rod at his side, and then he grasped the line trailing from the boat, and he pulled that; and the boat drifted; and the line remained taut, resolute, resisting him from the point where the lure had sunk. Weeds, the son thought, or worse, a log or a branch of a submerged tree. He gave a sharp tug. The line was now stretched parallel with the length of the boat. He tugged the line again and felt the tension give, and he smiled, pulling the line back hand over hand, it heavy with the weight of the lure and the snarl of weeds, and then he noticed that his father was staring down at him, standing in the rear of the boat, his face shaded by his cap. The son looked up at his father.

"I've got it," he said.

His father checked his cap and cast. The boat was even with the point now. The son could hear the noisy ducks.

The line lay in loops about his legs and feet. The weeds were bright green, brittle, slimy. As he pulled them from the line, their stems snapped in his hands.

"Need any help?" his father asked. With the tip of his blunt rod he was making two figure eights.

"Nothing I can't handle," the son said. He bent over his reel. "I've just got to unsnarl this."

His father laughed. "That's a good bird's nest." He turned away in the rear of the boat, then checked his cap and cast.

\*　\*　\*

*Sturdy, stocky, ever wary, the hungry hen feeds, up-ended, ever alert and aware of her brood, feeding in the water around her. The hen is automatic as the sudden flash of light and sound of splash alert her, bind each muscle in her sturdy, stocky body, save those of her throat; quickly she rights herself; her chest contracts; her mottled, horn-tipped bill opens; her call is long and rasping. Shrill, it freezes the ducklings—they too are automatic as they freeze—and then in response to the silence that follows the hen's call the brood remains frozen, and all is still. There is silence then. Then the hen again opens her bill and cheeps; the brood is drawn toward her; hen; the brood huddles around the hen. She is the center, the magnet. Beneath the mottled mass of feathers, individual hearts furiously beat. Again there is silence, and as the silence sounds the body of duck relaxes; the hen then quacks; webbed feet begin again to paddle; the circle widens; the body of duck expands; growing, outward; all swim; the circle ever*

*widens; the hen feeds; the brood disperses; the hungry hen again*
*up-ends and feeds.*

*   *   *

Four-five-six. Pause, seven.

He knew he wouldn't catch a fish, not here, today; the weather
was too nice for it. The sky has to be overcast, he thought, and
there needed to be a stiff wind. Or at least a breeze. He knew that
his son knew that too, but since his son was younger, the man
thought, he believed the rules did not apply to him. He had time
to ignore them. Or something like that. The father smiled. He
knew what he meant. He looked at his son.

He was bent over his reel, trying to unsnarl his bird's nest.
His red life preserver cushion lay carelessly at his feet. The father
opened his mouth to ask his son if he wanted to use his rod and
reel, but he checked himself. His son liked to do things his own
way. He didn't like to be given help or advice. He had always been
like that. There was no reason then to make the offer. Even if he
were to put down his rod and reel and say he no longer wanted to
fish, his son would not accept it, would not see it as something
the father wanted freely to give.

The man stood, checked his baseball cap, and cast again. It was
futile. Fish just didn't feed in mid-July at noon in shallow water.
No, they were fishing here because the son wanted to, had insisted they drift, go with the current, move more or less evenly
and parallel with the shoreline, letting things follow their own
course.

They should be anchored over a deep spot, the father thought.
The lake water would be cooler in the dark, heavily weeded
depths, and the fish would seek the coolness, and the bigger fish
would seek them, seek the fish seeking the coldest of all possible spots. That was how to fish for muskie at noon in hot July.
The father gripped his rod and cranked his reel as steadily and as
firmly as he was able.

That was why the best fish were the best. The father stared at the clear water before him and with the tip of his rod made two figure eights. The best muskies knew how and where to catch the smaller ones. That was why they were the best. Of course the biggest of these could never be taken; there wasn't line or tackle strong enough to take them into any boat. Even now, deep in this lake, it was likely there were muskies that went fifty, sixty, maybe seventy inches or more. No fisherman the father knew really wanted to tangle with one. They were just too good, too heavy, too dangerous.

He stood and cast, then counted, and as he slowly sat he checked his cap. Their boat had drifted beyond the point. The father could see into the nearby bay, could see a wooden pier lined with halved automobile tires, and against the tires, gently bumping them, an old boat; and beyond that the heads of swimmers, children, bobbing, splashing the blue water; and, enclosing them, a row of buoys, white, makeshift—plastic bleach bottles—and then the opposite shoreline and the tall, majestic stands of birch and pines.

The trip up from Chicago was always worth it, he thought. He stood and with his lure made a pair of figure eights, then touched the visor of his cap, like a good baseball pitcher, checking his cap before he looked in at the catcher's signals, looking out and into the clear water before he made his next cast. Ritual, the man said to himself. The four-hundred-and-fifty-mile drive up from Chicago; the car packed by ten the night before; oil changed, new filter, points and plugs checked; departing by five the next morning; and then the drive, the long, hot drive. The same point on the same road where the accident had nearly happened, where the power-steering line had suddenly snapped, spraying its thick fluid all over the engine; the front of the auto smoking so thickly he could not see; the wheel suddenly locked.

Fortunate there was no one else on the highway. Fortunate to have eased the speeding car to a safe stop. Pumping the brakes evenly, calmly, as if the road were covered with snow. Fortunate to have felt the snap and pop of gravel beneath the wheels. He knew he was safely off the highway then. The others in the back-seat, unaware, quietly sleeping. Asking what had happened when he woke them up. No time to answer—getting them up and away from the automobile, which he feared might explode. Other cars whizzing by on the highway, mere inches away. The smoke bil-lowing. Then the tow truck from Black River Falls.

And they didn't take him, he thought. No, they could have taken him for an arm and a leg, but they didn't. The tow truck hooked the disabled car, its hood open like a mouth, then dragged it along the side of the road to the small town and gas station. There they replaced the broken cable, filled the line with fluid, wiped clean the engine, put him and his family back on the high-way.

Now, each July, even though the station twice changed owner-ship and he didn't need the gas, the father still stopped there in Black River Falls to stretch his legs and top off his tank. Each time remembering what had happened. Imagining what might have occurred had he not been so lucky.

He wanted to say something about all of this to his son, but he didn't have the words, and besides, he could see that the son was still trying to untangle his snarled line.

So the father stood and cast, then touched the visor of his base-ball cap, patiently counting, then sitting. And as he reeled in the white line of his line as steadily and as consistently as he was able, he felt the sudden pull, the jerk, the simple shock of the quick tug of the fish pulling out and away from him his ready lure and line.

\*   \*   \*

*From between the gray shadows of submerged trees and weeds, ahead and now beyond and swimming; the shapes of leaves: spear, fan, arrowhead; tendrils and pliant fibrils; around and be-tween, then over, passing; in the cool current tasting; moving through the water as the water is being moved, moving, through*

*the long snout of the mouth until it is expelled, expelling the
wonderful and ever-changing water through the flaps of the two
curved gills; expunged, behind, eliminated; the cool tastes inhaled and at once dispossessed; simultaneously now inhaling,
discharging, intaking, breathing, expelling, tasting, following the
cool and wonderful taste*

*the line breaks as the yellow eye sees without volition the
fierce, sudden, crossing blur of a small, dark, glistening thing
moving, twirling, intersecting, spinning shiningly above the
sweet taste of the cool current; the mouth gapes without volition;
the strong muscle of tail curves; the body twists and rises, rising,
rises; the muskellunge rises, entirely without will; resplendent
striped green muscle; sharp teeth snap.*

*       *       *

"Set your hook," said the son.

Trying to be helpful, his rod, reel, and line still lying in loose,
open circles about his legs. He looked back at his father, then at
the empty seat between them. He moved to it quickly. His father
firmly held his bent rod, his bare feet braced against the side of
the boat. The reel's drag setting clicked a steady stutter. His father
held the rod steady, then pulled back on it when the clicking
eased, cranking the reel. "Easy," said the son. He reached out and
touched his father's shoulder.

Then he looked at the man: at the dark whiskers on his face,
at the man's chest and the hair that protruded from his father's
sleeveless shirt, then down at the two hands, holding the rod that
held the line which held the fish in the water. He could faintly
smell the man's sweat, and he wanted suddenly to touch the
man's two hands, but he realized of course that he couldn't do
that. The son looked back at the man's face.

That morning in their cabin he'd touched his father's hands.
They sat at the small kitchen table, the son drinking a mug of

coffee and smoking his day's first cigarette, his father across from him trying to tie a lure on his line. For a while the son watched his father's attempts, then reached across the dark table and took the man's hands into his own, directing the thin and nearly transparent thread of the line into the lure's silver and circular eye. The moment bore unexpected intimacy as well as sadness. It was the first time the son had taken his father's hands and made them do what they were supposed to be doing, with the same impatience the man had always used on the boy. It was the first time the son felt his father aging. Then the man sat back and said, "Well don't leave the job half done, now tie it." He stood and busied himself with his tackle box. So the son tied his father's lure onto the line.

"He's some fighter," the father was saying. He shifted his buttocks on the life preserver.

The son pulled back his hand. There wasn't much he could do now, he realized. His father knew how to handle a fish. He looked around the boat for the net. It was there, behind him, lying between the thermos jug of water and his father's sandals. He asked his father if he wanted a drink of water.

"Not now," the man said.

The fight was nearly finished, he thought. His father was steadily cranking the reel. First the fish makes his run, the son thought, unaware that the thing tugging at him is attached to something. The tugging is a nuisance or perhaps an amusement. Sometimes a fish merely holds the lure between its teeth, playing with the pull from the line. Then, when it sees the shadow of the boat, it decides the game is over and leaps and spits the lure out. But if the treble hook is set and its barbs have dug into skin or bone, it's nearly impossible to spit the painful thing out. The fish has to hope it gets lucky and is able to bite through the leader or the line. And if it can't, the struggle is only a matter of time, a matter of the strength of the line or the fisherman's endurance. It's never a fair contest, the son thought, because the hooked fish has no real chance of escaping. As long as the line holds, even the strongest fish is eventually pulled in. The son stared at his father. Then he carefully set the outside oar in its oarlock and rowed until his father's line was perpendicular to the boat.

"That's good," said the father, "that's very good, you're doing fine, good, now come in closer, good, now come in closer."

The son smiled though after a while he realized that his father was talking to the fish.

They netted it with little difficulty. Once the fish was inside the boat the father was careful to wrap the mesh of the large net around it so that it couldn't escape, and then, after opening his tackle box, he measured the fish and then took out a small wooden club—a toy that had once been the son's, a miniature baseball bat—and cleanly and mercifully struck the fish's green head.

There was no blood.

"Forty-two-and-a-half inches," said the father. He looked at the son and smiled.

The son nodded, then tried to light his cigarette. It wouldn't draw. He'd chewed the filter nearly through. He moved back to his seat in the front of the boat and took another cigarette from his open pack. All at once he felt badly for the still fish wrapped in the net. Regardless he said, "It's a beautiful fish. Congratulations."

His father was starting the motor. He turned and smiled. "Let's go to the lodge for a beer," he called above the sound of the motor. The son looked at him, and the father motioned. "A beer," he repeated. He raised his hand and tilted back his head as if to drink.

Near their pier the father slowed to share his news with a man in a nearby boat. The man was still-fishing. He cupped a hand behind his ear to hear the father, then gave a big thumbs-up. When the father asked him how his luck was, the man shouted, "Nah, no luck, just little crappies." He made a broad sweep of his hand.

There, floating sideways in the weeds, were several dead crappies. The man shouted that he'd caught them for the turtles and the birds.

"Have a beer with us," the father shouted. He wanted to celebrate his forty-two-and-a-half-inch muskie. He again motioned. "To hell with the crappies."

The fisherman in the small boat laughed. "We work fifty weeks a year, for what?" he shouted, then repeated his joke about fishing for the turtles and birds. Then he shrugged and cranked in his line and waved his hands again. "Sure, I'll let you buy me a beer."

As their boat approached the pier, the son said, "Didn't I tell you we should drift with the current?" He took the cigarette out of his mouth and smiled.

His father nodded. He maneuvered the boat alongside the pier, then looked at his son, smiled, and touched the visor of his cap.

\* \* \*

*Dropping from the cloudless blue sky to the still blue water, the great heron stretches its great blue wings and glides, long legs trailing, toes flexed, head and neck drawn back. The bright flashes shimmering in the water are familiar, recognizable. Fish. The bird is certain as its head and neck extend; as its eyes fix upon the largest of the floating crappies; as its long legs dangle, then stretch forward, downward; as the feathers of its tail spread.*

*The blue wings beat, beat, beat; the great bird hovers; the descent to the water's surface is certain, is complete.*

# The Language of the Dead

The fat Christian Brother smoked a Camel in the green room. Over his head was a row of sweating pipes. The basement room smelled fusty, like damp socks and unwashed T-shirts fermenting inside a locker, like seventh period always smelled, no hot water left in the showers. Vinnie stared at Brother Stanislaus, then at the wall, last year's team, league champions, in a silver frame. Next to that hung a cockeyed picture of the Blessed Virgin, a bunch of flowers in her hands, her head tilted toward the team's picture, or toward God in Heaven above, Vinnie thought. He fidgeted, a grin glued across his face. Behind him on the door's opaque glass were the black backward letters: ECIFFO SEHCAOC. Vinnie turned and read the letters, and they said something else. Something frightening. A phrase unintelligible. Like the blackboard in Brother Damian's Latin class, Vinnie thought. Exactly like Latin, Vinnie concluded, just like what Brother Damian said was the sacred language of the dead.

Brother Stanislaus paced the room, coughing, his stomach jiggling beneath the folds of his black habit. Vinnie looked at the rolls of fat, then put his hands to his own stomach. It pushed out just a bit against his belt. Beer, Vinnie realized. Too many Saturday night six-packs with the boys. He felt guilty. Only fifteen and already with a belly, he'd have to do some jumping jacks and sit-ups. He despised calisthenics since they always made his head swim. Stanislaus turned and blew a cloud of smoke in his face.

"So what did you tell them?" The voice was harsh as gravel. It was exactly like it sounded when it rasped over the PA.

Vinnie grinned. "Nothin', Brother." He swallowed, and his ears popped.

Brother coughed. Vinnie had been dreading this all day. You

didn't get called down to Brother Stan's office just for nothing. Brother Stan meant business. He was a mean one, maybe the school's most vicious. He punched kids roaming the hallways all the time for no reason. Brother Stan didn't need a reason, and if you were stupid enough to ask him for one he punched you again, but this time harder, and then he squeezed the tender pressure point beneath your shoulder blade until you nearly cried.

"Cow droppings," Brother Stan was saying, "pure and unadulterated cow droppings. I'll ask you just one more time, Vinnie. What did you tell them?"

Vinnie could see his own face reflected against the wavy backward letters in the glass. The boy shook his head. "Nothin', I tell you. I didn't tell them nothin', and that's the truth, I swear it." He suddenly wanted a cigarette bad.

Brother Stan turned slowly, smiling. "Have it your way." He reached for another Camel from the pack lying open on his desk. "Then it's an easy enough matter. First we'll call your parents and tell them that you've been suspended from school." He looked into Vinnie's eyes, spitting a piece of tobacco from his lip. "Your old man work for a living, like the rest of us?"

"Sure," Vinnie said. "He's a bricklayer. Union."

"I guess he must have to lay a lot of bricks to pay for your school."

"I work too," Vinnie said quickly. He felt defensive. He'd heard too many jokes in his life about his father's job, and plus he didn't like for anybody to think he had to depend on anybody. He found himself staring up at the row of sweating pipes.

Brother sat down behind his desk. "Where?" he asked.

"At this drugstore, Kerwin's. I run deliveries and help out in the back." He wondered if Brother knew that he also helped himself to Kerwin's cigarettes, stealing them regularly by the carton. And sometimes candy and soda, and once a naked girlie magazine. But Brother Stan couldn't know about all that. Or could he? Vinnie wondered. He didn't know what all Brother Stan really knew.

The man had covered his face with his hands, as if he were tired or about to claw out his eyes. The hair on the back of his fingers was thick, like an animal's. "So what did you tell them, Vinnie?"

"Nothin'," the boy repeated. "I'd tell you if I'd of said something. You don't want me to make up a lie, do you?" His voice was shrill.

The Brother laughed. "Of course not, Vinnie." He paused. "After I talk to your old man on the phone I'll walk upstairs and write down in your records that during a basketball game you insulted two of our school's guests and physically threatened them, causing them and their friends to respond with a fight in our school parking lot"—he let out a sigh—"which resulted in their school's bus being damaged to the tune of over three hundred dollars." The hairy fist suddenly pounded the desk top. "Over three hundred dollars' worth of damage!"

"But it didn't happen that way," Vinnie shouted. Then he checked himself. He'd promised himself he wouldn't say anything. Nobody believed him when he told the flat truth, and when he made up a story he'd get all caught up in it, be turned all around and twisted so that he'd eventually contradict himself, and that was always worse. That happened all the time with his father. Then the boy caught the end of the bricklayer's belt. No, he was no good at lying. Like his father always said, when Vinnie lied it showed. He watched the heavily breathing Brother begin cleaning his fingernails with his matchbook.

"Then how did it happen, Vinnie?" The black chest moved in and out.

"Honest, Brother, I didn't do nothin'." Vinnie remembered the night he'd come home an hour after curfew. His father had been waiting at the door. Vinnie ducked the first slap, then said he'd missed his bus, you know how it is on Sheffield. Sheffield and what? his father roared. Why didn't you walk? No time to think, Vinnie didn't have either answer, he'd simply forgotten all about the time, drinking beer with his friends in back of the drugstore.

Listening to stories. Trying to have a regular time. Vinnie smiled, remembering his friends' reaction to the girlie magazine he'd copped, remembering all the jokes they'd told, the time they'd had—and then his father's slap knocked him back against the closed door behind him. I'll teach you to lie when you talk to me, his father shouted. Then the man took off his belt and let the buckle fly.

"What's so amusing, Vinnie?" Brother Stan was rising from his chair.

The boy shook his head. Either way, he was trapped. "All right, all right," he said, "I'll tell you how everything happened. You already got me suspended from school, so what do I care? I might as well spill the whole beans."

Vinnie wanted one of the Brother's cigarettes. He wanted one bad. He turned for a moment toward the door and saw the crazy black letters, then shook his head, feeling disoriented, short of breath. Seventh period must be over, he thought. They'd miss him in study hall during eighth. Brother Casimir always took attendance. Then Vinnie remembered where he was and why, and he thought again of his father, imagining his ma telling him the news that night when he got home. Dear Jesus, Vinnie thought. My life is finished with . . .

"Come on," Brother Stan said, "spill the beans."

Vinnie shrugged. "Well," he began, "we were at the JV game just minding our own business, and then when it was over we went downstairs to try to sneak a smoke." He looked into the Brother's face for a response, but there was none. "So when we got there these two guys came over to me and started telling me they didn't like the way I looked."

"And what did you say?" Brother lit another cigarette.

"I told them they weren't a pair of good lookers themselves, and then they started in on how their varsity team was gonna cream our team, just like their JV team did. So I said they were full of it. And I was right, wasn't I, Brother, because I heard won that game." Vinnie smiled, his thoughts for the moment light. "So then one of the guys, the bigger one, pushed me in the chest and told me that if I was looking for trouble he knew where I could find some. But I didn't do nothing back, and that's the truth, Brother. Instead I walked over to the guys and they asked me what happened so I told them about the two fellas, and the guys said that if anything happened they were right with me."

Brother Stan tugged the skin above his collar, making a rhythmic scratching sound. Vinnie leaned back in his chair.

"And?" Brother Stan said.

Vinnie let out a breath. "And then we went back upstairs to watch the varsity game. But when we got to the landing those two guys were just standing there, so I stopped and told everybody that these were the two clowns who were looking for it. So the guys said, these two? And then somebody pointed at one of the guys and said he'd better watch it. And then some more of the guys came over asking what was what, and let me tell you those two fellas were really shaking."

"Were there any punches thrown?"

"No, Brother. It was all talking. We had them circled, and they seemed pretty scared." Vinnie wet his lips. "It felt good, the guys sticking up for me like that. Like I was one of them. Then I went into the gym, back to my seat, and then just before the game started Brother Patrick came over and pulled me out of the stands. He told me I was kicked out of the building and put on suspension, and that I had to come to talk to you. I guess the two guys complained or he heard us talking on the stairs."

"And then what did you do?"

"I took a bus home, Brother. I didn't have nothing else to do."

"You didn't stay around for the fight?" He reached for a pencil and pad of paper.

"No, Brother. It was all talk. And it was pretty cold outside."

"What did you do when you got home?"

"I don't know. Watched television or something."

"What was on?"

Vinnie scratched his head. "I remember. Perry Como. My father really likes him."

The boy felt empty. It hadn't been that bad. Then the door rattled open and Mr. Kominski, the assistant principal, entered. Vinnie turned and watched him walk past the black letters. Vinnie read the words frontward and smiled. COACHES OFFICE, the letters read. He felt better now. He'd told the truth. Then the door banged shut, and Mr. Kominski looked at Brother Stanislaus.

"Has our young rebel confessed his transgressions?" The assistant principal stood behind Vinnie's chair, his hands lightly resting on Vinnie's shoulders.

Brother Stan laughed. "Oh, he's been singing his tune."

Mr. Kominski's hands moved to Vinnie's neck. "So who won the big fight?"

Vinnie didn't say anything. He wasn't sure if Mr. Kominski was speaking to him or not. But when the hands tightened and began to press against the nerves below his shoulder blades Vinnie attempted to face them. "I don't know nothin' about the fight," he said, squirming in the chair. "I went straight home after they kicked me out."

"You went home?" The hands continued to squeeze him.

"Yeah," Vinnie said. He stared at his feet. He was trying to control himself but he couldn't help it. He attempted to break away.

"Hold on," the hands said, "just hold on, I'm not hurting a big strong guy like you." The hand on Vinnie's right released its grip, but then came slapping hard against the side of the boy's face. Vinnie winced and braced himself.

He knew he'd be hit again. The only thing there was to do was to close his eyes and take it, without moving, like a man. With a little honor. Without saying anything. Never begging for it to stop. The hand was stroking his arm now, squeezing the biceps, and then when it let go it came rushing again to the side of his face. Vinnie squealed. His ear throbbed and burned. He pictured his father's brass belt buckle as it whistled through the air and down against him. It made a bright, painful sting. The other hand was still pressing the nerves left of his neck. The worst thing was to beg for it to stop. Vinnie hung his head, trying to place himself inside his shoulder's pain, and with the next slap to his ear he was able to crawl inside the space, and he visualized it — it was round and gold, like the sun or the tip of a lit cigarette, burning against his neck and brain. He had only to endure the beating — it could never go on forever — and then it'd be all over. He had only to outlast it and not to beg. When it passed there would be numbness, then a long stretch of time. Then only soreness, only a throbbing, an ever-present ache, everything sore and stiff. He knew the ways in and out of the space. If he removed all his clothing now he'd be able to see each of the gold belt welts — the boy could finger them gently, knowing that they'd eventually go away. Vinnie pictured himself leaning against the sink in the bathroom the last time after his father had beaten him — it had been early one evening, and the boy imagined watching his hand open the mirrored doors of the medicine cabinet, his arms and back still stiff with the burning pain. That was when he poured shaving lotion on his wounds, the bottle of Aqua Velva heavy and cold in his hands as he dripped a cool pool of blue liquid into the shallow of his palm. As he rubbed the lotion deep into his skin he nearly cried out it hurt so goddamn bad. But he continued, purifying each bruise and welt, after a while enjoying it, the sting, the cool sudden burning, the way it made his eyes leap open and tear, the way the pain so fiercely burned and throbbed. Vinnie enjoyed it because he deserved it, because he'd done something wrong. Sinned. Disobeyed his tired father. With his thick bricklayer's hands and broken fingernails. Who was only trying to do what was best for his son. Punishing him because it was for his own final good. Inside Vinnie's ear there was a ringing.

Something felt wet on his neck. Vinnie remembered how he'd walked out from the bathroom, silent and proud, his shirt hanging loosely over his shoulders and back, his head reeling, his father sitting alone in the front room, his stupid mother walking past him then in the hallway, stopping, sniffing the air, then asking him as if nothing was wrong if he was getting ready now to go out on some special date.

He was staring at the toe of a black shoe. It belonged to a white stretch of sock and the cuff of a black pair of pants hanging just below the hem of a midnight black cassock, stained with the grayish white of cigarette ash. The boy was afraid to lift his head. Midnight black, nightmare black. Vinnie's hand gingerly touched the wet upon his neck.

Was it blood or only sweat? His arm hurt as he moved it. Vinnie swallowed, and the thin, clear ringing in his ear went away for a second. But then it returned, and then the boy again felt the dull pain in his shoulder, and he saw that his two legs hung helplessly from the edge of his chair. He was dimly aware of voices around him, but he could not make out the words. The liquid on his fingertips was clear, so it had to be sweat. The sounds were foreign to him, like the Mass, like Brother Damian's Latin class.

Mr. Kominski stood behind the boy, reaching politely across the wooden desk to light Brother Stanislaus's outstretched cigarette. "So he went directly home, you say. Have you got anybody to check his story with?"

Stanislaus pushed his chair back from his desk. "Naw, but he wasn't involved in it, I'm sure of that. Pat put a good scare into him and he went straight home, so it could have been anybody's doing after that. You know how these things get started."

"Like a match on tinder." Kominski walked over to the picture of the Blessed Virgin. "That was quite an emotional game. I could hardly believe some of the calls the refs made." He stepped back, then straightened the dusty picture.

"It was all McGinnis," Stanislaus said. "For the first time in his life he really took control of the boards." Stanislaus tapped his cigarette in the ashtray that lay before him, then looked at it and emptied it behind him in a wastebasket.

Kominski wiped his mouth with a handkerchief. "How many

rebounds did our boy McGinnis take down? I heard Allegretti saying this morning it was nearly thirty."

"Twenty-eight," Stanislaus said. He smiled broadly. "And you know that breaks the Catholic Prep League record by two."

"That should break the city record." Kominski looked at the door.

"Well, we called all the stats in," Stanislaus said. "I'll get back to the papers and have somebody look it up."

"Still," Kominski said, "that was certainly some kind of game for only a senior in high school." He opened the coach's office door.

Vinnie looked up. There on the dirty green wall before him was the silver photo of the league champions, and above that the dark outline where a crucifix had hung. He looked down again. A strand of drool dripped from the side of his mouth. He was still dazed. He swallowed. His ear was still ringing. He inhaled sharply. Through the ringing he heard footsteps in the hall.

The ringing shattered, and Vinnie began screaming. At first there was no meaning to his sounds. Stanislaus moved quickly to his side, and Kominski stepped back into the room, the office door rattling shut.

The boy lay against the wall, recoiling from the Brother's touch.

"Hey," Stanislaus was saying, "get a hold of yourself. Come on now, Vinnie, get a hold of yourself, grab hold."

"Is the nurse still on duty?" Kominski asked.

Shielding his head with his arms, the boy thrashed his legs and continued to make incomprehensible noises, and then when Stanislaus pulled Vinnie's arms away and raised his own hand to brace the boy with a slap, Vinnie looked up and broke into sobs and began repeating the words, "Don't hit me, oh don't hit me, don't hit me, no, don't hit me."

Brother Stanislaus leaned back slowly and lowered his arm.

# The Man in the Movie

The siren whines. Whines. And whines, even louder. It is west of me, I think, on Ashland Avenue—two, three hundred yards away. I am thinking so clearly it amazes me. I should be in a sweat. I should slow my pace. Unwind, and try to walk more naturally. I don't want to attract any attention or make even the slightest mistake. I should stop looking around. There are so many sirens in the city, the chances are this one isn't for me. It might be only an ambulance, I think. That's right. I must think the siren is only an ambulance.

Then it already has its victim. Or is on its way to pick him up. I must believe this. It's got nothing to do with me. It's just somebody else's accident. Shattered legs, arms, and faces smashed by windshields. Necks gone snap against the side of glass. Or some poor woman having a baby. I pity the poor baby. To be born into all of this.

Now the sound's behind me. One hundred yards? I can feel it as it screams behind me. And even though I know I shouldn't, I stop and turn. To see it. Stare it in the face. Now the bright red light has grabbed me, and I'm rooted to this spot. Will it see me?

It *is* an ambulance. A Red Dart. Passing. Something lies propped up on its bed. I must relax. I'm safe now. Someone else was covered up with blankets and strapped down. Not me. I am not what is strapped down. It was someone else—a heart attack, a broken face, a sucking chest wound, or just an animal. Sure, a dog. I must relax, it's passed me.

Funny to think it was a dog. I am walking evenly now, and now my arms and back break out into the sweat. I expected that. It is a good, hot, prickly sweat, and I'm glad of it. I smile at myself for thinking it was a dog. But, now that I really consider it, who can tell? These days anything is possible. I must stop this rapid walking. If I slow, I can light a cigarette. I will, when I'm near the next street corner. I shouldn't stop now, here in the middle of the block. Ridiculous my thinking it could have been a dog.

But who can tell? I look around. This neighborhood is plush. Silent. High rises. I bet inside the lighted lobbies there are doormen. And private guards. Salute you when they see you, buzz open the door, maybe press the elevator button for you. Or, if you're like me, give you the fast one-two, then kick you out on your behind. Who can tell what really goes on inside? There could be apartments full of dogs, sleeping on the sofas, shitting up the places as if they're backyards. I bet if one of those dogs had a heart attack, the guards would call an ambulance. And as long as the owners have money, the Red Darts would whine and come. Why not? If you have money just about anything is possible. No demand is too outrageous. There are always people who are willing to do even more outrageous things to get some of it.

Didn't I see a movie once where some rich lady left a million to a tomcat, or was that the movie where the cat owned the baseball team? I tell you, since I got back I've seen plenty of movies. Not this trash in color, but the old classics, the ones in black-and-white. They've got them on now day and night. What else did they expect me to do after I got back but watch movies?

I'm walking slower now, and now my body is relaxing. Everything's going right, according to plan. Though I didn't expect that ambulance. I can see now that I should have. I'll walk down this street until I reach the El station. Then I'll be safe. I don't think anyone is following me. I know it'd be suspicious to turn around to check. The last thing I want is to act suspiciously. I can't afford to make any mistake.

Two more trees, the mailbox, then the street corner. I'll stop to light a cigarette. Here? No, two more steps. There. Protected by the mailbox.

Oh Christ, my jacket has been open. All this time. Has anyone

that it's cold, shiver, and zip your jacket shut. Act naturally. Catch the tiny silver teeth. Cover up your rookie shirt and your bulky rookie secret. Zip the damn zipper. All the way up.

Christ! What did I just get through thinking about details? Walking around with my jacket open, like a damn advertisement.

Like a son-of-a-bitching billboard. Am I stupid!

Now relax. Control your hands. Put them in your pockets. Get yourself under control. Think. Use your head. Go over the plan.

I'm still on my planned route. A half mile east of Ashland Avenue, with the El station just ahead. I haven't spoken to anyone. In my front pocket is my train fare—exact change—so I won't have to wait. In my back pocket is my lipped cigarette butt, pack of matches, my one burnt match. I have the take from the liquor store folded inside the flap in the sheet I've wound tightly around my waist. I have my weapon—a pearl-handled .38—inside the flap inside my jacket. Which I had left open, for anyone with eyes in the front of his fool head to see. Bulging conspicuously.

I'm sweating again. I hope it's a good sweat.

I'm no longer alone. Pause at the corner. The sign says DONT WALK. I want to run. Stay. There are too many others here. Is this Clark Street? Calm yourself. You knew you'd have to cross Clark Street. Go through the plan again. You are out for a walk on this dark, windy evening. With my jacket tightly zipped shut. You are just like the others, back in the world, home again. I'm home again. Home, and I saw a Red Dart ambulance, and inside it was a rich old lady's sick dog. Or was it the tomcat who owned the baseball team?

It was the Yankees. No, sweetheart, my name isn't Yankee. Yes, I'm American, but that's not my name. I was just thinking about being home. Pour me more of that gin. Come back to bed. Yes, I'll pay you again. You want to know my name? It's Babe— no, make it Gehrig. Lou Gehrig. I'm the iron man. Here, I'll show you. Come back to bed.

Is this Clark Street? Such a long, endless light.

You were daydreaming again. Snap out of it. I must snap out of it. Step lightly off the curb. The light is green. The sign says WALK. Don't mind the others. They don't care about you—they're just out for a good time. I like a good time, but I need money to have one. Then get a job. There are no jobs. There are plenty of jobs, you just have to find one. Turn off the TV and get up. I didn't know it was on. Look, it's on. I'm walking across Clark Street. The set isn't on. I'm not watching TV.

Be careful how you walk. Don't bump into the others. I'm walking a fine, straight line. Don't walk so slowly that you look as if you're loitering or are checking the corners for women or are looking for a good time. I'm not in need of a woman. I don't have enough money for a good time. I'm walking quickly across this street. Slow down—the car ahead is turning on the red. Let it pass. They can do that legally now. Stop now so that it can pass. Don't stare at the driver. Look instead at the dog in the backseat. Is that the ambulance? Keep walking.

This corner is too crowded. I smell a bar. Walk past it. But my throat has been so dry. Remember how you lipped your cigarette? Suck on your cheeks. Slow down, you're walking too quickly.

Hands in the pockets of my jacket. Shoes on the sidewalk, concrete, where they can't be traced. Leave no clues behind and they'll never find you. That's it, leave the others behind. You're home again, Chitown. *Shy-town*. That crowd wasn't looking for you, just waiting for a bus.

Should I take the bus?

You'll take the El. Remember the plan. Stick to the plan.

I'm better now. There are fewer of the others on the street. With each step the night grows darker. The air is filled with more wind. It was the others that made me nervous like that. I have never in my life liked crowds. Now I'm all right.

But what if someone saw you? And is calling the police?

Then I'll turn around and waste them. I'll stop right here and take out my weapon. Shouldn't I prepare myself? I could take it out and hide it in my pocket, with my finger, ready, on the trigger.

Don't be a chump. No one saw you. You're all right. Stick to the plan. It's a good plan. You thought of everything.

I thought of everything. I'm pleased.

Keep walking. That's it. Easy. There. Now look around. See, there's no one else out on the street. Turn around. No one is following you. No one has seen you.

I'm all right. Though sometimes I think my mind is getting soft. I saw a movie about that once. A rich woman began to forget things, such as where she left her necklace, what day and year it was, who she had invited over that night for dinner. Or am I thinking of something else? Wasn't it about a man who was trying to make his wife go crazy? I liked him because he had such a detailed plan. She really wasn't crazy at all. Finally she discovered him hiding upstairs. What gave him away was the flickering gaslight. He'd thought of every single thing but that.

I'm like the wife, not crazy. My shoes hit this good, firm concrete. They say details.

De-tails.

They're what make up this world. Life is made up of situations, and inside each exists a set of rules, and if you break one you have to pay for it. Fair enough, but the rules are always changing, like now with the right turn on a red light. You've got to keep up. I believe all this as much as I believe in anything.

My heart clatters in my chest. Calm down. It's that kind of world. It has to be. Because if it isn't like this, then what in hell makes sense? Why was Jake wasted and not me or the others? It can't be due only to blind chance. It has to be because he managed to deserve it. The night Luccio stepped on the land mine was just after he'd changed the laces in his boots. Don't tell me there wasn't a connection. They picked off Motor City the same day the mail caught up with us and he found out his wife had run off. Don't suggest that Motor City didn't go after his old lady in the only way he could. I've thought a lot about this, as much as I've ever thought about anything. I wouldn't want to go on living in a world that wasn't like this. That would mean that nothing you do is of worth, that there are no differences between me and the next guy. I can't believe that. When I was over there I used to hear so much bullshit, guys saying that when your number's up, your number's up, as if you couldn't do one damn thing about it. I just can't live by that. When your number's up it's because you forgot a detail. Because you and you alone messed up.

It must be like that. It can't be any other way.

Take tonight for example, with the old man in the liquor store. I walked in and pulled my weapon, just like I'd planned, and then I set down the rules. The old man broke them. I told him clear as day to keep his hands up. And as I turned, he reached down. Going for the alarm, pulling his weapon, scratching a damn mosquito bite on his leg—why he reached down isn't important. What's important is that I said to keep his hands up to Heaven until I'd left. So I squeezed off a round. I had to. I would have expected the same from him if our situations had been reversed.

I had checked out the store beforehand, knew when it was busy and when it was not, knew that he didn't padlock the back door so I could make my escape through there, knew that the first thing the cops would look for would be a clue, so I left them one, my ski mask, inside a trash can in the alley, after I'd stashed the take inside my shirt, and I knew exactly where I should walk and where I shouldn't, what route to follow, and as soon as I am on the El, after giving the woman in the cage exact fare, I'll be home free, invisible in the city. I know that the cops will be trying to trace the ski mask, so I left them a common one, the kind they sell at Goldblatt's. I picked it up last Christmas Eve.

I know they're checking it for clues this very moment. They'll find what they're looking for, hair, long dark strands of hair, from the wig I have on my head, which I purchased at Sears Roebuck, pretending it was for my sick, self-conscious wife.

Pregnant, I told the salesgirl. Losing a bit on the top.

I must say, I am laughing. I checked everything. I did everything right. Again I know how this world works.

But you did forget to zip up your jacket.

Then I should have been noticed. Then someone should have seen me. Who? One of those doormen? The driver of the Red Dart?

But no one saw me. I'm right here. One hundred yards or so from the El station, one hundred yards from safety. Surely no one saw me make my one, small mistake.

But are you sure? What if someone did see you? What if it is all really due to blind, stupid chance?

Since you overlooked a detail, you deserve to be wasted. Since you broke one of your own rules, you know you'll have to pay. The old man in the liquor store paid, didn't he? Jake, Motor City, and Luccio paid. The man in the movie paid.

But what if no one saw me?

You're still guilty because you still made the mistake.

I'm dizzy. It's because of these crowds. I'm approaching the corner beneath the El. There are too many cars here for me to avoid looking at all of them. There are too many others here around me. They stand in groups, talking, excited. It's too much. I must slow down. I must stop my hands from shaking.

I'm nearing the movie theater. The lights beneath the marquee are bright. What if someone asks me for a cigarette? What if someone wants to know the time? I'm not wearing a wristwatch. Should I guess? Should I pretend I'm a foreigner and don't understand them?

I don't know what I'm doing. I have just taken off my Sears Roebuck wig. No one is noticing me, so now I unzip my jacket—there—and now my hands are poised on the buttons of my shirt. I unbutton my shirt. There's a good amount of sweat on my chest. I think it is bad sweat, the kind that makes your mind stop thinking. The kind that freezes your insides and makes you want to clutch your sides and throw up.

I want to throw up.

Now I am calming down. Did I just vomit? I'm not sure. My hands are wet with something. A group in the crowd beneath the lights stands looking at me, and now one of the women is pointing. She sees the sheet that is wound around my waist. She turns. Now she is speaking to the others.

I feel pleased. The world is recognizing me, and it's not because my number is up but because I'm making mistakes now, deliberately. I hear a dog barking. Vicious barks. The world is noticing my mistakes.

I know now what I'm doing. I've just stripped to the waist. And now I bend and reach inside the secret flap inside my jacket, which lies on the shining sidewalk beside my laced boots. And as I unholster my weapon I think of Jake and all the others and the man in the movie, and suddenly now I'm relieved.

# The Daughter
# and the Tradesman

S he lay in her bed, pretending.

She knew she wouldn't be bothered if they thought she was still asleep. Their sounds were harsh and sudden: one of the aluminum chairs scraped against the kitchen floor, the heavy frying pan slammed the top of the stove. Soon she would smell coffee. Bobbi knew their routine well. She tried to sleep through it each Saturday morning. If the girl listened carefully now she would hear the clanking plates her mother was carrying in from the cold pantry and the tin sound of the cheap radio her stepfather played in the bathroom. Sometimes he sang while he shaved. Or tried to sing. Then he would begin clearing his throat and his nose. Each time he spat into the sink was like a slap. The refrigerator door banged open, then closed. There was the clash of the silverware drawer. Her stepfather spat again. It was disgusting.

She would be foolish to expect better, Bobbi thought, hiding down beneath her sheet, because her stepfather was a disgusting man. Unlike her father, who was dead now. Her stepfather was common: he chewed his food with an open mouth; his fingers were short and thick and always filthy from the dingy little shop where he repaired broken radios and clocks that ran too slowly and rusting toasters that were too tired to pop up. He boasted regularly that he could fix anything. The house was littered with things he claimed he'd fixed, things abandoned by their original owners, things with retaped wires, soldered cracks.

She turned her face to the wall. She wouldn't end up like her mother, a middle-aged woman whose flesh sagged from her body and whose teeth were made of plastic. Was that what false teeth were made from? Bobbi thought. She ran her tongue along her own teeth. Her mother's mistake was that she'd married again; she'd settled for a second-rate, common man. Bobbi shivered. If there was one thing she had learned, she thought, it was that she must never settle for anything less than the absolute best. She believed her father had understood this. He had been born in Europe and was a gentleman. He was a Lithuanian. He came from the aristocracy. He had the best of blood. And that blood ran in her veins too.

Beneath the thin sheet Bobbi stretched her body. It was young and lithe. Her Baltic ancestry had given her fair skin and hair that was light brown, and her features were slight and rounded. She was proud of herself and her body. She was fifteen, and she knew that when she wanted to she could be beautiful.

Her beauty would be her escape. Bobbi had a boyfriend, a boy named Tom, a good and reasonable boy from Granville Avenue far up on the North Side, a much better section of the city. Tom was straight and dark and tall. And he didn't go to Lake View, the public school where she went, where the swarthy Uptown greasers and the dumb bucktoothed hillbillies and the Mexicans and all the Puerto Ricans went. Tom went to Holy Cross College Prep, out in the suburbs, and he was in the upper fifth of his senior class and co-captain of the boxing team. He was the nicest boy Bobbi had ever known. It made her feel so important and so proud to wear his ring on a chain around her neck to Lake View. The ring allowed her to ignore all the vile city boys—she could look down on them—and all the girls she knew were oh so jealous of her.

She heard water in the sink. Her mother rinsing the dishes, leaving them for her to wash. Bobbi had her duties. Her stepfather said that as long as she lived under his roof and ate his bread she would have her duties. Of course her mother agreed with him. She said work was good for a young girl. Sometimes Bobbi hated them.

She shifted onto her stomach and reached beneath her bed. The dress and the needles and thread were still there. She would wear the dress today. Soon her mother and stepfather would leave for the shop, and then Tom would sneak over, and before that she would carefully shave her legs and bathe. Bobbi had planned it for so long. She wanted everything to be perfect. She had fixed the dress's hem so that it just brushed the tops of her thighs, and she hoped that when Tom saw her he would think her beautiful and sexy. Bobbi had rehearsed her movements and lines. Acting blasé and nonchalant she would tell Tom that she wore the dress all the time, sometimes even to school, once even when she had to give a class report, and then she would show him how she had looked when she'd sat in the dress up on her teacher's desk—she would smile and sit demurely on the dining room table—and all of this plus the new perfume she would wear and the expressions she'd put on her face and in her eyes would make Tom jealous and excited and he would love her, and then they would *do it.* And then Tom would never leave her, ever, because he was such a clean, decent Catholic boy and because she would have given him what all the boys wanted. No, he would never leave her. And then he would finish school and she would finish school and they would be married—maybe even on her birthday—and she would wear a veil and a white dress, and she would never have to live another day with her mother and her stepfather. Tom would never regret anything. She would make a perfect wife. And then for the remainder of her life, for the first time in her life, she would be happy.

There was a pounding on her door. Quickly Bobbi turned to face it. She called out, "Yes?"

"We're leaving," her mother shouted. "It's eight o'clock. Wake up, or were you planning on sleeping all morning?"

"No," Bobbi called back, slipping out of bed. She hadn't realized it was so late. "Good-bye," she said. "I'm wide awake."

\* \* \*

"Well," Tom said, "who was it?"

Bobbi slowly looked up from a spot near her knee where the new razor blade had nicked her skin and a dark clot of blood had formed. Her hand moved to cover the spot. Her legs were crossed. She was sitting on the table in the dining room. Tom stood in the front room, facing her. The late morning light from the windows behind him framed him.

"I'm sorry," Bobbi said. "Tom, what was what?"

"Whose desk did you sit on?" Tom blinked several times, and then his Adam's apple jumped as he swallowed.

Bobbi put her hand over her mouth and laughed. She thought quickly. "Oh," she said, "it was Mr. Percy, he teaches algebra." She didn't know why she had chosen Mr. Percy; he was short and drab, and she disliked math. There was something in Tom's voice as well that she did not like. Her fingers picked at the scab near her knee. Maybe, she thought, she could tell Tom she did it for a better grade if he asked why. She waited for him to ask why.

"I thought you didn't like math," he said instead.

"I don't," she answered. She was irritated. Sometimes Tom could be so stupid; he couldn't even tell when she was lying. Now the lie was becoming more of a problem than it was worth. But there was still plenty of time in which to mend things, she thought. Her mother and stepfather wouldn't return for hours.

"Then why did you do it?" Tom asked. He stared at her, then folded his thick arms.

He was still at it. Couldn't he see? Boys *were* stupid. She wanted to get down from the table. She wanted to sit with him on the sofa and be held by him, but she felt unable to move. She felt pinned. She looked at the vase of plastic flowers on the end table. Shaking her head she finally said, "I don't know, Tom, I just did it."

"You just did it?" he said. He sounded like he was spitting.

"Yeah," Bobbi shouted, "I just did it." The tone of her voice frightened her. She felt as if she wanted to cry. "Look at me," she said. "Tom, please look at me."

He had turned toward the windows. She slid off the table, smoothing her dress down across her thighs with her hands. Tom turned around, and she put out her arms to him, and when he didn't move she said, "Please come here and hold me, Tom. Please hold me. I'm cold."

"Then maybe you should put on some decent clothes." He turned once again toward the front windows, then stretched his arms and back.

"You're a bastard," Bobbi said, and she hoped that it would make him angry because now she was angry and because everything she had so carefully planned was going astray. She thought about how long it had taken her to shorten the dress, and how she'd had to hide it and the thread and needles from her mother, who never left anything private in her room. Her mother sometimes even opened her personal letters and listened on the extension when she talked on the phone. Her mother treated her as if she were an infant. It was unbearable. Bobbi was furious.

She glared at Tom's broad back. "Did you hear me?" she shouted. "I just called you a bastard. Aren't you going to say anything to me, you damn bastard?"

He looked at her and laughed. Bobbi saw that she had gone about this entirely wrong, and for a moment she felt ridiculous.

"You did it for a grade, didn't you?" Tom was saying. "You dressed yourself up like a cheap damn tramp so you could get a better grade." He shook his head and made a hissing sound. "You could have come to me, you know. I'm good at math. I could have helped you."

Frustration rose from Bobbi's stomach and burned up through her chest and the back of her throat and behind her eyes, and before she was aware of what she was doing she had clenched her fists so tightly that her fingernails sliced into her palms, and then she began crying. She felt suddenly blinded and fiercely angry. Then she was aware that Tom had come over to her and was putting his arms around her and drawing her close to him, and she put her arms up around his neck and relaxed, all at once grateful that he was holding her. She felt relieved—she let out a breath and was crying less bitterly—and it was then that she recognized what Tom was doing, that instead of comforting her and forgiving her and understanding her he was trying to unzip the back of her insulting and ridiculous dress.

*        *        *

Her father, her real father, had been a tall dark man, thin, with large hands and an easy smile, an indolent laugh. By trade he was a salesman. His name was Constantine Tzeruvctis, and even as he emigrated from the lush expanse of Lithuania he was willing to make a deal: the stony immigration officer stamped Constantine's papers but shortened his last name to Tzeruf; the exchange seemed fair enough. It was a big, new country. Constantine worked his way west to Chicago, sweeping floors, washing dishes, even polishing brass spittoons, and then for the next thirty years or so of his life he peddled Dr. Cheeseman's Liquid Wonder, a patent medicine. From door to door to door to door on Chicago's North Side the immigrant tradesman worked: knocking, smiling, selling.

All of this Bobbi learned from her mother, from the few photographs in the album and cardboard boxes on the hall closet's back shelf, from the yellowed newspaper clippings that described her real father's death. And like a detective in the paperbacks she read and the late-night movies on TV she had seen, Bobbi had attempted to piece everything together. More than anything she wanted to know, to understand. But of course that was impossible. There were pictures missing from the album. There were questions her mother refused her the answers to. And the musty clippings from the newspaper dumbly reported only the *what* of the situation.

The girl knew facts about her father. That he drank. That occasionally he attended professional baseball games, preferring Charlie Grimm's Cubs. That he wasn't overtly religious. That both his birth and his death days fell in September. In the oldest photos her father smiled and sported a moustache. His discharge papers from World War I listed his vocation as Tradesman and his character as Excellent. His complexion had been Fair. Next to *signature of soldier* was a neat, curly *X*, and beneath it was printed "His Mark." Bobbi kept the papers in her top dresser drawer along with her jewelry, her letters from Tom, and her cosmetics.

In her parents' wedding photograph Constantine sat, her mother stood. As a child Bobbi had thought that her father was sitting because he was dead in Heaven. Later she realized it was custom. Her mother's hands gripped the back of the chair. Her father's eyes looked down at his shoes. Neither smiled.

The first child, a girl, had been stillborn. She was not named. The gray tombstone in the cemetery read BELOVED BABY TZERUF. Green fans of lichen grew inside the letters. Bobbi was born eleven years later and was named for Robert, her mother's grandfather.

By then Constantine was nearly sixty. But when he was younger, oh, he had been quite a fellow. Bobbi's favorite story about him took place one warm summer evening on the Near North Side in an area then known as Bucktown. Bucktown was a tough, tooth-and-nail Polish neighborhood, so named because back then many of its residents owned goats. Constantine was young and ambitious, knocking on doors, a dark bottle of Dr. Cheeseman's Liquid Wonder in his hand when suddenly from the street a shotgun roared. Constantine shielded his head with his suitcase. The lead shot was meant for him. He was not hit, but a lantern hanging from the frame house was, and the wooden porch caught fire.

Constantine began to beat the flames with his jacket. Then the door of the house opened, ever so cautiously, and the barrels of another shotgun looked out at the tradesman's face. He raised his hands and started to explain. He showed them the contents of his suitcase. He pointed to his now-smoldering jacket. He placed blame for the incident on the Italians or the Negroes. The men of the house then summoned him inside. While the women tended to his scorched jacket Constantine took out his wares, and before he left Bucktown that hot, humid evening he had made over a week's worth of sales.

Bobbi liked the story because in it her father was such a wonderful liar. Only a Lithuanian gentleman could lie so boldly and get away with it, she thought. She didn't realize that the patent medicine her father sold for nearly half his life was so worthless that men would try to kill him. Bobbi's mother agreed that it was a fine story. She said it showed how clever Constantine was—he could turn tragedy into success—and how quickly he had learned to do whatever was necessary to get ahead and make a profit in America.

The newspaper clippings described a *dark deranged foreigner* on the downtown Washington Street subway platform *waving his arms and suitcase* and *causing a general disturbance.* The police were promptly called. There was *shoving* and *a great deal of noise and confusion.* The man *appeared to have been drinking* and *did not speak in English. It happened quickly,* one witness said. *The foreigner struck a policeman, Sergeant F. Mahoney, on the side of the head with a suitcase full of bottles, and then, when a second officer withdrew his revolver, the foreigner screamed and leaped onto the tracks directly into the path of a southbound Elevated "B" train. The conductor, Calvin Jefferson, testified that he could not stop his train in time. The police have launched a complete investigation. The body was later identified.*

This occurred in 1957, in September, when Bobbi was four years old.

*       *       *

There was barely time to hesitate—it was happening too quickly—there was barely time in which to think, but Bobbi realized that she was falling. She broke her fall with her left arm. Then she was on the rug, beneath the dark table, trying to make her escape. Around her was the thick clutter of chair and table legs. Tom held her, his arms circling her bare thighs. She tried to kick loose. She was afraid, yet curiously aware that in this time when she should have been terrified she was still thinking coolly, rationally; and as the hands pulled her back she felt strangely proud. She was still in control of the situation, she thought. She wasn't crying. She wasn't hysterical. She was still able to function and to think. With these abilities, she thought, she could handle this boy and his suddenly rude hands, this Tom, her Tom, quiet Tom, Catholic Tom, stupid, clean-cut Tom. He would stop if she wanted him to, she thought. He wasn't as bad as the city animals she had to go to school with. Why, all she would have to do would be to say *stop.*

So this was a game like all the other games, all the at-the-movies games and in-the-front-hallway games and oh-just-let-me-touch-you-for-a-moment tricks and twists. Bobbi thought about the many ways she could get boys to notice her at a dance, the way the boys fumbled in their pockets for a match to light her cigarette, the way they cleared their throats before they tried to speak, the way they pressed up against her, trying always trying to get a little further, a little closer, somewhere they had never gotten to before, when all she had to do was to change the way she smiled, to push a hand against a shoulder, to yawn into an eager pimpled face. Oh how they stopped. Cold. Flat. Bobbi knew boys, how they stopped; deflated, tumbled, put down, down, down. Oh, how the boys would tumble. Boys were such silly prissy pampered things, and just as long as she stayed away from the gutter types she could control them, tease them, wind them clear around her little finger, and they loved it. How they loved it. They always came back to her for more because they truly loved it.

How she hated them. Boys were so weak and easy, and finally so boring; how easy it was to predict what they would do. Tom straddled her, kissing her neck. How she truly hated him. She drew a breath and in a clear voice said, "Tom, stop."

He grunted, pawing the front of her dress.

"Tom," she said, "Tom, please stop and get off of me."

Again he grunted.

She pushed against his shoulders with her hands. He slapped her arms away easily. When she pushed against him again he grabbed her wrists and pinned her hands over her head against the rug, and she realized how much stronger he was. She considered whether or not she should physically fight him. She stared up at the chandelier hanging over the table. A spider web floated between two of the bulbs. If she struggled, she thought, he would have to stop. Wouldn't he? Wouldn't he stop if she struggled?

Then all at once she started to cry, thinking not so much that he was hurting her now or that she was so afraid, but simply that it had now come down to this, this abject humiliation, this pushing and grunting, and now she would lose both him and something she had always felt was an important part of her.

Behind that there emerged something deeper, a scary feeling. The girl felt for the first time that she understood something about her father, and she pictured the old tradesman. She imagined him walking wearily from door to door, and as she felt the sharp sudden pain of Tom's weight pressing against and into her she pictured her father wildly waving his suitcase down in the dark bowels of the Washington Street El station, and she thought this was how he must have felt when he killed himself. The boy's body above her heaved and jerked. She felt his breath against her face. This was how he felt, how empty and dark. She relaxed then, holding in her cries. Even though her eyes were tightly shut, her tears continued to run from them. Her tears were hot and searing as they streamed down her cheeks into her ears and hair, and then the boy's body finally came to rest, heavily and silently, upon her.

\* \* \*

She lay in the bathtub and began to wash herself.

At least it was over, she thought. He was gone. He couldn't

have left more quickly if he'd tried. Lying on the rug, her eyes still closed, she'd heard him zip his pants and stand, then open and close the front door. He'd said nothing. What do you say? There was nothing he could say. Not even *sorry*. She thought bitterly that he could save his apology for his Catholic confession, and she smiled, imagining him penitent, kneeling and beating his chest in some dark church. The bastard. It was ludicrous.

For a moment she pretended she was washing herself with holy water. She prayed that the water running into the tub would make a miracle. "Holy water, holy, holy water." Turn me back into a virgin, lift the stain from the dining-room rug, lift the pain, the memory.

She felt broken. Her insides ached. Then she began to shake her head, thinking that now she was the one who was being ludicrous, talking to ordinary bathtub water in a dark bathroom on an afternoon when she should be doing her chores around the house. She still had the morning dishes to wash, the kitchen floor to scrub. She could take care of the stain by spilling a cup of coffee or cola on the rug. She would tell her mother and her stepfather that it had been an accident. It would be all right. Sure. She was all right. It wasn't an expensive rug.

She shut off the faucet, sighed, then stood and reached for the light switch above the sink. The fluorescent bulb made a tinkling sound, and then the radio hidden inside the medicine cabinet blared: too loud and too tinny, violins and singing, a man crazy in love. Her stepfather's latest doing. He must have wired the radio to the light switch. Bobbi stood and shut both off, and as her fingers hovered over the knob of the radio she was startled and terrified, realizing that she might have electrocuted herself standing in the water in the tub.

The warm water embraced her as she sat. They had never found out exactly what it was that had killed her father. If he'd touched the subway's third rail before being run over by the train, he would have been killed by that. The third rail was electric. Once

Bobbi saw a gang of boys on the Armitage Avenue El platform trying to hit the third rail with their spit. They yelled for her to watch them, saying that their spit would sizzle. It made her cry, and after that she always took buses. At the hospital one of the city workers told her mother that if Constantine had brushed the third rail even with his palm, his death would have been immediate, painless. The worker had meant to be comforting. The train had severed one of her father's legs and crushed his head.

Did it matter? she wondered as she washed.

She would have lost her virginity anyway. It was bound to happen, sooner or later. The pain inside her would still hurt even if it had been someone trying to be tender, someone she loved. Death was still death. Her father still would have died. If he hadn't touched the third rail, the train would have killed him. If he hadn't jumped onto the tracks, maybe he would have crossed Washington Street and been hit by a car. Or been shot while being robbed. There was crime everywhere. There was crime even in the halls of her school. She could have been attacked behind the school or in an alley or in a gangway. She could have been knifed and killed. Her father could have eaten poisoned food or been killed in a brawl in a tavern. Death was still death. He could have contracted some ugly, hideous disease . . .

No, she thought. She held her body perfectly still. Nothing moved. There was no sound. No, what happened mattered. She'd made a mistake, trying to trade herself. And now there was no one to fix her.

She looked down at her legs. She pretended they were broken. She imagined her entire body was paralyzed because she'd accidentally touched the subway's third rail. And now was the moment when her great efforts would allow her to move. She tried to wriggle her toes in the water. Yes! She was doing it! It would be in all the papers. She was cured! She slowly rotated her right foot, then her left foot. She bent her knees. Moved her head, her hands. A complete recovery.

Bobbi looked at the sink, the toilet, the gray walls. She was aware that she was acting silly, and she tried to laugh out loud at herself—she was kicking her feet now and flexing her arms and splashing sheets of water out of the tub—but instead of laughter a bitter cry came from deep inside her. Bile rose in her throat. The girl's cries echoed terribly in the small, darkened bathroom.

# World without End

G loria in excelsis Deo," Peter said as he steered his squeaking Chevy down Hampton Boulevard, a Winston bouncing on his lip. Glory be to God on high. It was a Sunday morning, Memorial Day weekend, the beginning of the tourist season. Most of Norfolk's residents and visitors were eating breakfast or still in bed, asleep. Lena and August, who had flown in from Chicago on the discount airline the night before, sat next to Peter on the car's blanketed front seat. Lena wore a black hat and was as thin as a bird. Gus was gray and as round as a house cat. "Et in terra pax hominibus bonae voluntatis." And on earth peace to men of good will. The old Chevy groaned as it rumbled down the street, tires delving into every pothole. From behind a large cloud the sun tried to shine.

"I'm so glad my boy still knows his prayers," Lena said, patting Peter's bony knee. He was wearing blue jeans and an open-necked blue shirt.

"You need new shocks," August announced. His hands firmly gripped the dashboard. "We'll never make it to church in one piece. This is worse than a roller-coaster ride."

Peter glanced at his parents, exhaled a thick stream of smoke, then shook his head and smiled. "Laudamus te. Benedicimus te. Adoramus te." We praise thee. We bless thee. We adore thee. Pleased with himself, Peter braked and downshifted as the car neared a red light. So far the visit was going well. He idled in neutral. And he'd do whatever he could to make things stay that way. "Confiteor Deo omnipotenti," he said, nudging his mother. I confess to almighty God. Peter beat his chest three times and said, "Mea culpa, mea culpa, mea maxima culpa." Through my fault, through my fault, through my most grievous fault. The Chevy lurched forward as the light turned to green.

"My Petie," Lena laughed. "He's giving us the whole Mass." She turned from her husband's frown and faced her son. "So you're a regular parishioner at this church, Petie?"

"Sure, Mamma." Peter flicked his cigarette butt out his open window and looked away.

"It's a nice church we're going to, not one of those new ones that look like a gymnasium?"

"Beautiful," Peter said, eyes on the road. "Stained glass everywhere you can see. More statues than a cemetery, even more than Chicago's Holy Name. So gorgeous that when you walk inside, it takes your breath away." The Chevy hit another pothole.

"This ride is taking my breath away," Gus said with disgust.

Peter and Lena ignored him. "But not so beautiful as our parish back home," Lena said. A furrow of worry creased her brow.

"Of course not, Mamma," Peter said. "Nothing can ever beat what's back home."

Lena adjusted her hat and beamed.

"A church is a church," Gus said. The blanket beneath his legs had begun to bunch up, revealing the tips of two springs that poked through the upholstery. "What do you think, God cares about the furniture?"

"God cares about furniture," Lena said.

"Yeah," Gus said, "maybe the collection basket." He pounded the dash and laughed.

"He cares," Lena said. "Why else did he make Jesus a carpenter?"

"Two points, Mamma," Peter said. He licked two fingers and slashed them in the air.

His father's thigh discovered the exposed springs. "Petie, you really got to do something about this car. How can you take a girl out and expect her to sit on this? She'll rip her dress."

"Father Luigi still asks about you," Lena said. She shook her head at August, then pointed out his window at a magnolia tree. "He says, 'And how is Petie, good old Petie, my favorite altar boy, how's Petie now that he left his good parents and moved down to the South all because he didn't look hard enough for a job in Chicago or maybe because he just wanted to get away from his poor mamma—' "

"Father Luigi says all that?" Peter said.

"Every Sunday, Petie," Lena answered. "He stops us special just outside church. And sometimes when we see him on Thursday nights after he meets with the parish council."

Peter tried a different street. "You're a deacon now, Papa? Mamma said something about Father Luigi asking you to become a deacon?"

Gus wrestled with the springs, his thumbs trying to push them back beneath the upholstery.

"Eucharistic minister," Lena said. "And he doesn't think he's worthy." She smiled at her husband, then tried to still his hands. "He gets up and reads the Gospel sometimes, but he doesn't want to give out Communion. Why should he, he's no priest."

"Things change, Mamma," Peter said. "That's legal now."

"It used to be a mortal sin," Lena said, "and now they even let Nick Guiliani touch the Host." Nick Guiliani owned the neighborhood Shell station. "Whenever I see him passing it out with his greasy hands I change lines. Don't we, August? Holy Communion should come from a priest, not Nick Guiliani."

"Before you open your mouth, Mamma," Peter said, "you could whisper, 'Hey Nick, fill her up!' "

Gus chuckled as Lena said, "You take it in your hand, Petie." She held out her palm cradled in the other. "I'll do it the old way with Father Luigi, but when I get stuck in a line with an ordinary person I take it in my hand. You don't know if they wash."

"It still goes in your mouth," Peter said.

"Yeah," Lena said, "but I give the germs some time to jump off." She nodded and looked at her palm. "We talked all about it one night during parish council. Your papa thinks I'm crazy."

"What did Father Luigi say?" Peter asked.

"He thought she was crazy too," Gus said.

"No, he didn't," Lena said. "He changed the subject. Whenever

I talk to him lately, he changes the subject. That was the night he first asked me about you."

Peter turned back toward Hampton Boulevard. Azaleas in all colors bloomed in front of the houses lining the streets. Rhododendrons nodded their shaggy heads. Absently Peter said, "So what did you tell him about me? Good things?"

Lena stared for a moment at her hands, then at her lap, the car's roof, the dashboard, the floor, out the windshield, all the time shrugging and looking hurt and sad. Peter realized his error. He gave the Chevy gas.

"What could I say, Petie?" Lena let out a long sigh. "What can a mother say? That her son doesn't think the upstairs flat is good enough for him, His Royal Highness, so he has to move out into a dangerous neighborhood full of hoodlums and ends up wasting half of his paycheck on rent?"

"Mamma," Peter said, "that was two years ago."

"Let me finish," Lena said. "You asked me a question, so the least you could do is have the decency to hold your breath until I'm finished." Peter reached across the dash for another cigarette. August's thumbs again fought the springs. Lena nodded her head and smoothed her dress. "That's only the tip of the iceberg, my son. Don't think anything you ever do escapes your mother's eyes."

"Lena," Gus said, "get to the point."

"Don't be in such a hurry, Augusto," Lena said. She called her husband Augusto only during arguments. "You're on vacation now. You unloaded trucks fifty weeks for this. Relax. Remember, the doctor told you you don't have a strong heart." The Chevy bounced over another pothole. "Your son throws away his good money on an opium den on South Halsted and you don't think his mother sees? Then he met that girl. That stewardess. That hussy."

"Lorraine wasn't a hussy," Peter said.

"She moved in with you, didn't she?" Lena said. "You didn't marry her, did you? What do you think, I was born yesterday? I don't want to open old wounds, but you had only one bed in that apartment, Petie."

"You'd actually take a girl out in a car like this?" Gus said. He had succeeded in getting the springs beneath the upholstery, but the last bump popped them out again. "I can't believe it. I wouldn't be caught dead. She'd have to wear a suit of armor."

"Dominus vobiscum," Peter said. The Lord be with you. "Et cum spiritu tuo." And with thy spirit. With his right hand Peter made a broad sign of the cross over the steering wheel.

"But then she got wise," Lena said, "and never came back from that flight to Albuquerque."

"Tucson," Peter said.

"What's the difference?" Lena said. "You gave her some thrills, and the hussy packed her bags. So you had your fun, some pleasure, a little enjoyment."

"Please," Gus said, "it's a Sunday. Don't describe."

"It's only natural, Augusto," Lena said. "We raised a healthy boy. His blood is red like everyone else's. Just as long as he doesn't get a disease. Don't pretend to be such an innocent."

"The church is around here somewhere," Peter said, taking a drag off his cigarette and letting out the clutch.

Gus pointed to his heart. "Me? Pretend to be an innocent? Lena, I'm more faithful than Lassie. You believe too many of Monty's stories."

"I know you served your country faithfully," Lena said, "but you were stationed in France for two years. I go to movies. I'm a modern woman. I wasn't born with blinders on my eyes."

"Maybe it's the next block," Peter said. He exhaled a thick line of smoke.

"I've never strayed," Gus said. "Even before I met you I was faithful. I swear to God. Nowadays I don't even look."

"Oh," Lena said, "I could see what Little Miss Airlines was doing to our Petie." She turned to her son. "First you grew that ugly moustache. Then you started wearing those stupid clothes.

How can you sit down when your pants are that tight? And you wouldn't button all the buttons on your shirt. Was it the thin air up in the clouds that made her think that was sexy? Then you lost so much weight I thought we'd have to put you in the hospital. Didn't she know how to cook? I know you had a stove, I cleaned it with my own hands. But I suppose the kitchen was too far away from the bedroom."

"Lorraine was a vegetarian, Mamma."

"I cook vegetables. August, tell Petie that I cook vegetables."

"Petie, she cooks vegetables."

"What you need is to come back to Chicago where you can meet a good clean Catholic girl," Lena said. "Somebody like Rosamaria D'Agostino."

"Mamma," Peter said, "Rosamaria D'Agostino joined the Carmelites. She teaches kindergarten in South Bend."

"Are you sure you know where this church is?" Gus said.

"She would have married you if you'd have asked her," Lena said. "God was her second choice."

"There's a church," Gus said, pointing beyond the windshield.

"That's a post office," Peter said, "and Rosamaria D'Agostino wouldn't have married the Pope. Even back in second grade she wanted to grow up and become a saint. The rest of the kids talked about being cops or firemen or astronauts, but not Rosamaria D'Agostino. She'd even picked out her own feast day." He made a turn at 38th Street and tossed his cigarette out his window.

"Some children are blessed with ambition, Petie," Lena said. "Others need a little more time to grow, to settle down, mature. You could take a page out of her book, you know."

"But you always told me someday you wanted grandchildren."

"You could make plans, Petie."

"I know," Peter said. "Wake up, smell the coffee."

"The early bird eats the worms."

"Remember the Alamo," Peter said. "All the way with LBJ. Tippecanoe and Tyler too." He turned the wheel, heading back toward Colley Avenue. "Benedicamus Domino." Let us bless the Lord.

"You had such promise, Petie," Lena said. She snapped opened her purse, then shook her head sadly. "Three merit badges short of being an Eagle Scout. Second soprano in the fifth-grade choir. Sergeant of the Saint Felicitas patrol boys. Captain altar boy. Then in high school you were president of the Camera Club. We were so proud. And all of your science projects, Petie. Remember how you used to cut up those ugly worms? We still keep your jars and ribbons in your old room." Lena held a round mirror before her face as she spread on a fresh layer of lipstick. "Remember how proud we were when they printed the news of your honorable mention in the parish bulletin? We thought maybe you'd get a college scholarship. We thought you'd find the cure for cancer. Work with test tubes and one of those fancy electronic microscopes, go to your job every day wearing a white coat and tie. Ahh, a mother's hopes and dreams. I knew they were all down the drain the day you flunked out of junior college."

"I dropped out, Mamma."

"We're family, Petie," Lena said. "You got all Ds and Fs. Don't be polite."

"I wear a tie to work, Mamma."

"You wear a tie," Lena said. "The crazy Albanian who runs the fruit stand up on Clark Street wears a tie." She put her mirror and lipstick back inside her purse. "Whenever the ladies come in he smiles and pinches the cucumbers." She blotted her lips with a tissue. "That's all that men think of nowadays. I tell you, son, that girl ruined your life. Just look at you. Why can't you at least shave off your moustache?"

Peter braked suddenly at a red light on Colley. "Papa," he said, "did you ever feel like giving someone we know and love a little punch?"

"Petie!" Lena said, one hand flying to her breastbone, the other brushing the top of her black hat.

Gus stared out the window, then turned to Peter and smiled. "That's a good question. Don't think I was never tempted. But what good would it do? I'm not a brute. I once knew a man who hit his wife—remember Sal, Lena? The time he raised a hand to Sophie? We visited him in the intensive care. He couldn't carry on a conversation because of all the tubes running out of his nose and mouth. We'd stand beside his bed and say, 'Hello, Sal, we hope your bones set, we hope the doctors can stop the bleeding. The priest is on his way to give you Last Rites.'" Gus laughed. "They were boring visits. All Sal could do was gurgle." He caught Peter's eye, then nodded at Lena. "A man lives and learns. Are you taking us to church, Petie?"

"Of course, Papa." Peter revved his engine. "Why?"

"Because unless I'm seeing things we already drove twice past this post office." He pointed again beyond the windshield.

The Chevy roared across the intersection. Lena stared straight ahead, her arms folded atop her purse. She seemed made of stone or ice. The engine popped and whined as Peter put it through its gears. "There are an awful lot of post offices down here in the South, Papa," Peter said. "And every one looks alike. I figured I'd take the scenic route and show you some of the sights. We'll get to the church in no time."

"Messenger boy," Lena said finally.

"What?" Peter and Gus said, surprised.

"Messenger boy. Flunky. Lackey. That's what I brought into this world. A stooge. Big deal, so he wears a tie, maybe even a nice pair of dress pants, not that he puts them on when I come a thousand miles to see him. So he has clean hands. But he's still somebody's errand boy."

"I'm a courier, Mamma," Peter said.

"You're one of the Three Stooges," Lena said. "The stupid fat one they hit all the time in the face. Oh, I never liked that show. And I never liked those Marx Brothers either, honking their horns at innocent women and walking all over good furniture and throwing pies in your face." She took a deep breath. "So your papa should hit me? I'll show you hit, Petie boy. Pull over. Augusto, hand me your belt. He's not too old to beat."

"But Lena, the boy didn't mean anything—" Gus began.

"Augusto, he showed disrespect." Lena swallowed. "Take us to the airport, Petie. We're going home."

Peter drove, his mother's words falling around him like slaps. In the sky above a pair of seagulls squealed and soared. "Mamma," he said, "Mamma, I've always tried to do my best. It wasn't my fault I couldn't find a job in Chicago. Believe me, I looked. I tried. But when Lorraine didn't come back from Tucson I felt devastated." He glanced at his mother to see if she was softening. "Mamma, I was hurt. I was abandoned. I was lonely and without love."

Gus rolled his eyes. "There's a church. Or is it another post office?"

The Chevy bounced forward, free of stop signs, red lights. "I thought about becoming an alcoholic," Peter said, "and then I considered trying marijuana, paint thinner, Coke with aspirin. At night I walked the dark, rainy streets hoping I'd get mugged. I was broken and shattered, Mamma. I even thought about committing the unforgivable sin of suicide. I figured I'd cross State and Madison in front of a taxicab or I'd blow out the pilot and put the oven on broil."

"There's one," Gus said. "No, it's Southern Baptist."

"I thought about swallowing razor blades, Mamma. Jumping off the Hancock. Going to a White Sox game and telling everyone I liked the Yankees. But then one night I heard a church bell ringing, and I thought about your love."

"Go on," Lena waved. She unsnapped her purse and drew out a tissue.

"Yeah," Peter said, "it was noon and the church bells—"

"You said it was at night," Lena said, blowing her nose.

"Episcopalian," Gus said, "or else a fire station."

"I mean it was midnight, Mamma, and I felt so low I could have gone into a grocery store and eaten a jar of ready-made pasta sauce."

"Ugh!" Lena said. "I wouldn't feed that dreck to a cat!"

"Your love saved me, Mamma."

"So that's why you moved away?" Lena said. "Because of my love for you? Petie, you don't make sense."

"No, Mamma, no, I moved to get experience. They told me at all of the job interviews that I didn't have enough experience. Someday I'll move back."

"Catholic, Petie!" Gus shouted. "Roman Catholic! Look, a crucifix and everything! Stop the car!"

"Petie," Lena said, "why didn't you ever tell me?"

Peter jerked the wheel over, tirewalls scraping the curb. "You never asked me, Mamma. You assumed it was because of Lorraine."

Gus pushed open his door and was untangling his legs from the blanket, his trousers from the springs. Lena patted her son's head. Even though the engine was shut off, the Chevy knocked and sputtered and coughed.

"She was a nice girl, Petie," Lena said, "maybe a little too thin and stuck up with her nose in the clouds, but she was a pleasant girl to talk to. Still, she wasn't the right one for you."

"I know, Mamma," Peter said, "but a man's got to have experience." He helped his mother slide out of the car.

"You'll have to tell us more about your job," Lena said. "You deliver important things, like telegrams and legal contracts?"

"Not telegrams exactly, Mamma," Peter said. "Actually I deliver interoffice communications. But my job requires responsibility and punctuality."

Lena smiled. "Those are nice things, Petie."

"Mass starts in five minutes," Gus said, returning to the car. "Is my hair combed?" He tapped his wife's elbow. "Do I look all right?"

Lena licked several of her fingers and smoothed her husband's hair. "It's a nice church, Petie, not one of those ugly new ones?"

"It's beautiful, Mamma." Peter had never seen the church before. "I come here every Sunday."

Lena laughed. "Of course you do. Starting today." She pinched his cheek until it turned red. "Right after Mass we'll introduce ourselves to the pastor and sign you up." She smiled, then turned to her husband. "August, don't waste so much time. We don't want to walk in late."

Gus wagged his head.

"Walk on this side of me, Augusto," Lena told him.

"Coming, Lena," said Gus.

"Introibo ad altare Dei," Peter said. I will go unto the altar of God. "Ad Deum qui laetificat juventutem meam." To God who giveth me joy to my youth.

"And you walk on this side, Peter," Lena said. She smiled. The bright morning sunshine spilled their long shadows across the sidewalk. "I want us to enter the church together, like one big happy family."

Their shadows swam together as Peter took his mother's arm, then kissed her cheek. "Sicut erat in principio, et nunc, et semper: et in saecula saeculorum." As it was in the beginning, is now, and ever shall be. World without end.

# *Ladies' Choice*

A lot depends on your type of jacket—what neighborhood in the city you come from, what side of the dance floor you stand around, who you talk to, who talks to you. There are girls here who say no right to your face and others who sort of look you up and down and then kind of laugh. You can tell them apart easy enough just by looking at their hair. The dooper girls wear their hair down, most of the time parted down the middle. They look like they've just washed it. When they dance it swings around behind them in clouds and waves. The greaser girls always wear their hair up—teased, ratted, and sprayed. It never moves when they move. You have to be careful dancing with them because sometimes that spray gets into your eyes and makes them tear something awful. They're the ones who look at you sideways and smile to themselves.

Though you can never really tell. The number of city girls here at the dance is always getting smaller, or at least it seems like that. Girls' hair keeps getting longer, and sometimes it seems like everybody is washing it and combing it down the middle. So you just guess and make your shot.

But like I just said, what counts is the jacket. The doopers wear all the strange kinds. They wear lumber jackets that look like big red-and-white or black-and-white checkerboards, and they wear CPOs that look just like lumber jackets but without the squares. Then there are jackets that look like coats the kid's mother bought him so he'd have something nice to wear to funerals. Only the real numbnuts wear those, and if they're smart they take them off and carry them over their arms, or better yet they stash them in a corner and hope somebody walks off with them. You don't usually see guys with coats back at these dances week after week. None of the girls will have anything to do with them.

Sometimes I'll be walking around, like I am right now, and I'll see a group of guys find one of these kids' coats wadded up in the bleachers like a furry ball, and I'll watch the guys pull it out and go through its pockets, and then maybe one of the guys will have to spit, so he'll do that in the lining, and then another of the guys will hock on it or blow his nose, and then somebody will kick the coat out onto the dance floor where another guy will step on it and then kick it further out, and after the dance on the way out I'll see the loons asking the priests if they have seen their coats anywhere, and it's funny and pathetic and really kind of sad. I know these guys have probably never been to this kind of sock hop before, and after the experience they probably won't be back either.

See, everybody wears their jacket, and if you ever take it off you tell your friends to guard it with their lives. The priests and the men from the Fathers' Club and the Holy Name Sodality check your shoes upstairs in the gymnasium balcony. It costs a quarter, and they do it because they don't want their basketball court all scuffed up. They don't touch jackets, even like now in the middle of winter, because they don't want the responsibility. Plus, nobody would check their jacket anyway. A guy wears his jacket to show everybody who he is.

The greasers wear suedes and leathers. Expensive threads. They come from all over the North Side of the city, sometimes even from the suburbs, though usually the greasers from the suburbs are crazy, wanting to get into fights all the time. They're almost as stupid as the kids who wear their mothers' coats, and you can tell them easy from the city greasers because try as they might they never exactly look right. They're always a step behind, wearing what we wore yesterday. They're the greasers whose pants look brand new when we're washing them out or their hair is still long while we're getting closer cuts. They don't exactly know what to say to you if you talk to them. The dead giveaway is if they smoke filtered cigarettes or use a lighter. Most greasers I know from the city never use lighters because lighters always leak that fluid out through your pants pocket and onto your leg, and then you get a round red sore spot like a ringworm. I had a lighter once—a good one, a Zippo—and it did exactly that. It was back when I was a kid. I threw the damn thing away or left it in my locker at school or gave it to a girl or something.

I first started coming to these dances last year when I was a sophomore. They're the only thing really going on in the city on Sunday nights. I had to show them my ID from school to prove I was a Catholic. You don't have to be a Catholic to get in, but Catholics pay fifty cents less. Then all that fall and winter I came here every Sunday night, taking the Clark Street bus south from my corner and transferring west at Addison by the ballpark, then getting off at Western Avenue and walking north. I know it would be more direct if I transferred at Irving Park, but I like going past the dark empty ballpark and then walking by Riverview on Western and Belmont. Riverview is the amusement park, the largest and greatest in the whole world. Not that I've been to any others, but that's what people say. From the street you can see the Ferris wheels and the Pair-O-Chutes tower and that good long dip of the Silver Flash roller coaster. You can hear people screaming from the Wild Mouse and Shoot the Chutes, and wave to the folks up on the Space Ride. LAUGH YOUR TROUBLES AWAY announces the big billboard. I like walking past the sounds and smells of the place, and I especially like all the bright lights.

Coming here to the dance is something I do every Sunday. It's a habit, I guess, but it's a good habit, and I like riding the buses sitting in the back row looking out at all of the different people and the city, and I like walking the extra mile or so past the big shining used car lots, with the prices painted on all the windshields, and then by Riverview there's always something going on outside the main gates, somebody showing off or laughing their troubles away or trying to sell you something, and then past that there is the big public school, Lane Tech, and the rest of the walk to the dance is dark and quiet and peaceful.

Some of the guys told me once that Lane Tech was built on top of a garbage dump, and they said every year the school building slips down just a little and that by the year 2000 the whole place will have sunk and be filled in with water from the lake. I think about that every time I walk past the place. It sort of makes you wonder about what kind of ground it is you're walking on.

There's a guy now who's fast-dancing with a girl out in the middle of the floor, and the guy's big toenail is sticking out a hole in his sock. The greasers are around him in a circle, getting on him. What a stupid dooper, wearing a ripped pair of socks to a sock hop. The girl is looking down now to see what's causing all the commotion, and now she's blushing and walking right away. The dooper keeps on dancing. He shrugs and says to all of us, "Hey, knock it off, these are the socks I wear on Sundays." So a greaser asks him what he means. The guy says, "These are my holy socks," and I tell you that's pretty funny.

I guess I'm what you'd call a regular here, since I know mostly all of the guys. We hang around in the far corner, looking at people as they walk by. After we've checked them out, we start cruising. The outer fringes of the gym are filled with groups of guys just walking around checking things out. We look for genuine heartbreakers or girls we've never seen before or especially good dancers or jerks who're making fools of themselves.

The last are easy enough to spot. Some of these doopers must have learned to dance in Spazland by the way they flop their arms and kick their legs, and now just in front of me some bozo is whirling his lumber jacket over his head like he's a helicopter or something.

We're on the lookout for the mythical group of pretty girls, which is kind of like searching the forest for a bunch of unicorns. Everybody in the world knows there's no such thing. Groups of girls are like everything else—there are one or at the most two good-looking ones and the remainder are dogs. None of them will dance with you unless all her friends agree to dance so every now and then you have to make the sacrifice and dance with a dog. What you do then is get it over with as mercifully as possible.

But first there is the talking. Every group of guys has to have a talker—you know, somebody to walk over and break the ice. You need a face man—a guy who's good looking—to attract them to the guy delivering the spiel. I'm usually the third man, so I usually ask the third-best-looking girl, who is usually quiet, like me, and not a particularly high scorer in the looks department. As we dance we trade names and high schools and maybe streets where we hang out. It's hard to really get anywhere if you don't talk much. So after the song's over we just nod and kind of mutter thanks and see you, and I move on along.

The songs are records, 45s, that somebody, probably a young priest, plays over the PA. After a while you learn there is a kind of pattern to them. The sock hop begins with a lot of fast numbers, and the girls dance mainly with themselves while the guys just walk around, watching, and then there is a slow song and we make our first move then to get a dance, and then there are more fast songs and then a ladies' choice. In my time coming here I only got asked to dance once on a ladies' choice, and it wasn't a very pretty girl who asked me. She held me an arm's distance away and talked my ear off, saying I looked like her cousin from somewhere in Indiana who'd got himself killed in some kind of car crash, and I didn't say anything. I just danced with her. And when it was over the guys really kidded me.

Sometimes when I'm on the bus going home I think about these ladies' choices. I have a whole thing worked up. I'd be just walking around by myself, like I am now, and then I'd see a real pretty girl with nice long hair parted down the middle, and some guy would be bothering her, a real jerk, and then over the loudspeaker there would be the announcement that this song was a ladies' choice. The girl would turn to me then—there'd be a big smile on her clean, pretty face, and her big eyes would look up at me—and I'd stand tall and nod. Then we'd dance. The jerk would watch us. Then I'd ask the girl if the jerk was bothering her, and she'd say yeah, and I'd tell the jerk to get lost. And if he didn't move quickly and there was a fight I'd beat the crap out of him, and the girl and several of her pretty friends and all the guys would watch me, and even if the priests and the men from Holy Name and all the jerk's friends broke it up and kicked me out and took away my card for good it still would be worth it because of course I'd wait for the girl outside and take her home. At her door I'd hold her hand and kiss her lightly on the lips, and I'd take her out the next Friday night—we'd go all out and go to Riverview—and I'd tell her as we rode the twin Ferris wheels and Bubble Bounce and Flying Turns and Crazy Dazy and Bobs and Strat-O-Stat and Tunnel of Love all about how I'd heard that Lane Tech was built on top of garbage, and we'd figure out together what that means, and we'd talk and really get to know each other, and we'd touch and kiss, and she would be my girl.

Of course that could never happen. It couldn't even happen in the movies. In the first place, the only girls who like me are greasers, the girls with the dark, dark eyes and the miles of makeup, all the hair spray and thick, too-sweet perfume. They know me like they know their brothers. They can see I'm not a jerk or a tough guy, that I'm quiet, even shy. It's just no good, going with these girls from my neighborhood. Sure, I date them and take them to movies at the Uptown or Riviera and afterwards buy them french fries and Coke, but I don't like talking to them and I'm afraid that if I get involved with one of them I'll end up having to get married to her, and that'll be the end of my life. Then I won't get any farther than the corner bus stop, and I'll be just like the rest of the goons who work in the filling stations and supermarkets and corner drugstores, and I don't want that. I don't know exactly what it is that I do want, but I know it isn't that. So I walk past the greaser girls on the dance floor, looking for that pretty long-haired girl.

But the dooper girls are afraid of my jacket. I wear a leather, a Cabretta. It took me two months of working in the paint store unloading cartons of gallons of paint and sweeping up at night to pay for it. In my neighborhood everybody wears a leather jacket. Mine's a fine one. I take perfect care of it. After I bought it before I even wore it outside I rubbed the leather with oil to make it soft. A leather jacket can last you the rest of your life if you treat it right. The dooper girls won't have anything to do with me, or if they do I soon realize they're playing games, just showing off in front of their friends. Afterwards when their parents pick them up in their big new cars that sit double-parked outside the gym every Sunday night the dooper girls will be talking about the greaser boy they danced with, how the cat had him by the tongue, how he didn't know what to say, and they'll laugh and feel important and daring because they'd done something they thought was dangerous, slumming with a greaser boy, and they'll talk about it all week long in their high schools out in the suburbs, and if I see them the next Sunday night at the dance they won't even remember it had been me.

The guys from the city hate them. They act like they think they're better than us. Sometimes when we dance with a group of them we can tell they're making fun of us behind our backs— they have these signals to one another, and they double-talk with words you can't understand. I walk away from them then, frustrated and angry, not knowing what I'd done or hadn't done, not understanding really what just took place or why it has to be this way, these differences, why they exist. And if I look back at them sometimes I can see them laughing, and then when I see them upstairs in line waiting to get back their shoes they treat me as if I'm a stranger.

So I go to these dances not really expecting anything and always being very careful if I dance with one of the pretty suburban girls. Most of the time I just hang around with the guys in the far corner, and we talk and talk some more, and whenever one of their boys walks by us in his silly lumber jacket we make noises with our mouths and call him sissy, jerk, fairy, queer, and every now and then in the bathroom there's a fight, like there was earlier tonight—a group of greasers beat up a dooper, or maybe it was the other way around. Blood's red regardless. I go into the brightly lit bathroom for a leak and see a smear of watered-down blood in the sink, and there's blood splashed all over the urinals and up on the wall and on the floor, and then when I come back out I hear the talk of a fight after the dance in the park.

This big greaser comes up to me and says that some dooper had gone out with this girl who was going steady with a guy who's in one of the local gangs, and then he promises there'd be a big mess after the dance tonight. I say, "Sure." He says, "We'll stomp their damn heads." I say, "Of course we will." He says, "It's us against them," and then he slaps me hard on my shoulder, and I nod and he shakes my hand as he walks away. I begin my circles around the dance floor, looking for that pretty long-haired girl.

My socks are wet and cold from all the snow people have tracked in from outside. The guys in the far corner stand around me joking, talking about tonight's fight. I don't remind them that Chicago's finest are always outside, sipping coffee in their squad cars. The guys know this. All of us know this. The big rumble's just talk. The only thing that's real is the blood in the bathroom, and who really cares about it if it isn't yours, if you aren't the one bleeding in the ambulance or the back of the squad car. I want to say all of this to the guys around me but I don't. I'm tired of talk tonight. So I tell the guys instead that I think I'll take a rain check on the extracurriculars and go home early, get a little sleep or maybe just sit around and watch something on TV.

The street outside has that special quiet that only a heavy snowfall gives the city. Everything is muffled and softly edged. As soon as I am out in the air I feel better, stronger. I walk directly toward Irving Park. My shoes sink quietly into the deep snow. Normally I'd head south so as to walk past Lane Tech and

Riverview, but it being winter the amusement park is closed for the season. Its bright lights are unlit. I walk, not really thinking about anything, and now I see the lights of what seem to be squad cars, and I move slower, wondering what's happened in the park.

A policeman calls to me. "Hey, you," he shouts. "Stop."

I turn. A policeman is running toward me in the snow. Behind him are more squad cars. I hear the wail of sirens in the distance.

"Freeze," the policeman says, and I smile, thinking I don't need a cop to tell me it's cold out. I slow and turn, and the cop grabs my arms and throws me to the ground. He calls me a punk and kicks my side. I hold my stomach and draw my knees up to my face. The other policeman takes his club out and shouts for me to put my hands behind my back and stand. As I do, he shoves me toward one of the squad cars. The cops push me against the warm front grill.

"Hands on the hood," the cops holler. "Spread your legs."

My heart pounds. I look at my breath hanging before me in the air. The cops unbutton my jacket and frisk me down, then jerk my arms behind my back and cuff my wrists.

There's someone inside the squad car. The first policeman opens the door, then leans inside and talks. I try to look at him but the other cop pulls me over to the opposite side of the squad car, and then someone rolls down the back window.

It's the girl of my dreams, the one who picks me. She leans forward in the backseat and looks at me. Her white coat is splattered with blood. Beside her is the guy who must be her boyfriend. He's crouched down, his hands covering his face, the bright red of his blood pouring between his fingers.

"Is he the one?" the cop behind me asks. He pulls down hard on my wrists, and when I say it hurts he kicks my leg and tells me to shut up. The other policeman shines his flashlight on me.

"Is he the one?" the cop says again.

The boyfriend leans back and groans, then starts to throw

up. His vomit comes out from between the fingers of his hands, splashing against the back of the front seat and then down onto his legs and his red-and-white lumber jacket.

"I don't know," the girl is saying. She's really really pretty but she looks so scared. Blood shines in her long, straight, blonde hair. "I think so. He could be." She bites her bottom lip. "Yeah, it's him. I'm sure of it. He's wearing the same jacket."

The cop behind me pulls back on my wrists again and pushes me away from the car.

The sirens are nearly upon us. All I think of is Riverview, its darkened towers and lights.

# *Idling*

Sometimes when I'm hauling I drive right past her house. The Central Avenue exit from the Kennedy Expressway, and then north maybe two, three miles. The front is red brick and the awnings are striped, like most of the other houses on Central Avenue. Her name was Suzy and she was the kind of girl who liked cheese and sauerkraut on her hot dogs. She was regular. She went in for plain skirts, browns and navy blues, wrap-arounds, and those button-down blouses with the tiny pinstripes all the girls wore back then. She must be as old as I am now, and the only girl ever to wear my ring. She was special. Suzy was my only girl.

I met her at a party at a friend's house. A Saturday night, and I was on the team only I had pulled my back a couple of days before—too serious to risk playing, they said, sorry, we think you're out for the season. I'd been doing isometrics. And though they gave me the chance to dress and sit with the team I said the hell with it, this season's finished, get somebody else to benchwarm with the sophomores.

Which was OK, because the night I met Suzy the team was playing out in Oak Park, and had I gone I'd have met my father afterwards for some pizza, like we usually did after a game, but instead I went over to Ronny's. The two of us hung around the back of his garage, talking, splitting a couple of six-packs, with him soaking out a carburetor and me trying to figure if what I had done with the team was right. Ronny told me stuff it, if you can't play you can't play. There are things nobody can control, he said. You just got to learn to roll with the punches. He was maybe my best friend back then and I was feeling lousy, here it was not even October and only the second game. Let's get drunk, Ronny said, laughing, so I said stuff it too, there's a party out in Des Plaines

tonight. So we got in his car and drove there. Then some of the
game crowd got there, all noisy and excited, and I met Suzy.

It went real smooth and I should have known then, like when
you're beating your man easy on the first couple of plays you
should know if you've got any sense at all that he's gonna try
something fancy on you on the third. I started talking to her,
thinking that since I was a little drunk I had an excuse if she shut
me down—maybe I even wanted to be shut down, I don't know, I
was still feeling lousy—but she talked back and we danced some.
Slow dances, on account of my injured back. And when I told her
my name she said you're on the team, I saw you play last week.
I said yeah, I was. She seemed impressed by that. But she didn't
actually remember that it was me who intercepted that screen
pass in the third quarter, and damn I nearly scored. She smiled,
and I held her.

Things went real fine then. We danced a lot, and later Ronny
flipped me his keys, and me and Suzy went out for a ride. Mostly
we talked, her about that night's game, and me about why I'd decided not to suit up, which, I told her, was really the best thing for
me. There's something stupid about dressing for a game and not
playing, I said. If they win, sure it's your victory too, but what did
you do to deserve it? And if they lose, you feel just as miserable.

I took her home then and told her if it was OK with her I
wanted to see her again, and all the talking made me sober up,
and that started it.

I don't know if you ever had duck's blood soup. It's a Polish
dish, and honest to God it's made with real duck's blood, sweet
and thick, and raisins and currants and egg noodles. Her father,
the father of three beautiful little girls, with Suzy the oldest, took
all of us out to this restaurant on north McCormick Street and
ordered it for me. He said the name in Polish to the waiter, then
looked at me and winked. He even bought me a beer, and I was
only seventeen. The girls watched me as I salted it and kept ask-

ing me how it tasted. I didn't understand what was the big deal. I said it tasted sweet. Then Suzy's mother laughed out loud and told me what was in it. I think she wanted me to be surprised.

Suzy went out with me for her image. There was no other reason, it was as simple as that. Now, there's not much glory in dating a former defensive end. I think Suzy went out with me because the year before I had dated Laurie Foster, and Laurie Foster had a reputation at Saint Scholastica, where Suzy went to school. This is where everything gets crazy. Laurie had a reputation for being fast, which I don't think she deserved, at least not as long as I was taking her out. We never really did much of anything, but because I had dated her I got a reputation too, and I never even knew about it. I guess there was some crazy kind of glory in dating and later going steady with a guy who had a rep.

She said let me wear your ring, hey, just for tonight, and I said sure, Suzy. And she asked me if I liked her and I said of course, don't you like me? She laughed and said no, I'm just dating you for your looks. I was a little drunk that night and she said do you ever think about it, Mike, I mean do you ever just sit down and think about it, and I said what, and she said going steady. I told her no. Then she asked me if I wanted to date other girls, and when I said no I didn't she said well, I think maybe we should then, and finally I said it's all right with me, Suzy, if you think it's that important, and she said it is, Mike, to me it really is. She wore my ring on a chain around her neck until she got a size adjuster, then she wore my ring on her hand.

Pretty much of everything we did then was her idea, not that I didn't have some ideas of my own. But Suzy initiated pretty much of everything we did for a while back then. Ronny was dating a girl who lived near Suzy out on Touhy Avenue, and I remember once when we were double-dating Suzy and I were in the backseat of the car just sort of fooling around and she said can't you unclasp it, and I said oh, sure. And that time we were at her house studying at the kitchen table—her mother was down in the basement ironing and her father was still at work—and she says not here, Mike, but hey maybe in the front room.

She said hold me honey, hey, and she touched me and I touched her and she was wet and smelled like strawberries and her mouth nipped my neck as I held her. She said Mike, do you like me I mean really do you like me, and I said yes Suzy, that's a crazy question, I really like you, and she held me then and made me stop and we sat up when we heard her mother coming up from the basement.

The next weekend I bought some Trojans, and Ronny lent me his car for the night, but before I went to pick her up the two of us got a little drunk in his garage. Ronny said I'd better try one first just to make sure they weren't defective. He said people in those places prick them with pins all the time just for laughs, and I said yeah, I sure hope this thing'll hold, and Ronny said there's seventeen years of it built up inside of you, and I said damn, maybe she'll explode, and he said she'd better not, not on my upholstery, and we laughed and he threw a punch at me and we drank another beer and then blew one up like a balloon and it held good and we let it fly outside in the alley.

The backseat was cold and cramped, and Suzy cried a little when it was over, and we wiped up the blood with a rag. It meant something, I thought, and I started taking going steady a little more serious after that.

It must have been the next month that her mother started in on me. She was young then and still very pretty for a woman who'd had three kids, but she began out of nowhere saying little things like here, Mike, take a chair, and did you really hurt your back or is there some other reason why you quit the team? I had always tried to be polite to her. Then Suzy started to get on me, asking me sometimes exactly what was I doing when I pulled my back, how was I standing, and couldn't I maybe try out for track or baseball or something in the spring? I couldn't figure where they were coming from, and I tried to explain that even before I got hurt I hadn't been that good a football player, that I'd been on the team simply because I'd always liked to run and play catch and go out for long passes with my father on fall afternoons. Suzy's father seemed to understand, and he'd tell me stories about his old high school team, funny stories about crazy plays and the stuff the players wore that was supposed to be their equipment, and then sometimes he'd get serious and say it wasn't a sport anymore at all, that now it was a real butcher shop, a game for the biggest sides of beef, and if he had a son he'd let the boy play if he wanted to but he'd hope his kid would have the good sense to know when to quit. Because all athletes have to quit sooner or later, he said. Everyone quits everything sooner or later. The trick is knowing how and when. Toward the end I got to know him a little. I'd go over there sometimes even when I didn't feel like seeing Suzy but when I knew there was a game or something else good on TV, and once the three of us, me and my father and Suzy's father, sat around and shot the breeze and had ourselves a really good time, and we must have drunk a whole case of beer, and Suzy and her mother ended up out by themselves talking in the kitchen.

Suzy's father asked me how I quit the team. When I didn't say anything he told me that once he had worked for a guy and after a while he saw plain as day that he was getting nowhere. He said even though they already had Suzy and needed every penny, one day he sat down with his boss and told him that he simply couldn't work there any longer. He said Mike, there are things sometimes that you just have to do, but you need to learn that it's almost as important to go about doing them in a decent way. I told him that maybe I had been a little hotheaded with the coaches. He said he respected me for what I did, on account of it showed that things mattered to me, but maybe staying on the team and picking up a few splinters on the sidelines might have been a better way to go about doing it.

I knew even back then that me and Suzy weren't going to last long, and then I started realizing that what we were doing was serious business, especially if Suzy got pregnant. I was cool toward her then. It was around this time that I found out from the guys at school that she had gone out on the sly with another guy. This guy, she told me when I asked her about it, was her second cousin who was having a little temporary trouble finding himself a date. I laughed good at that and said damn it, at least if you would've told me I wouldn't have had to hear it from the guys, and we both found out then that I really didn't much care. We had a long talk then, and then for a while things went OK.

For a while. Until May, until I was walking down the second-floor hallway at school and I got wind from Larry Souza, a guy who was dating one of Suzy's friends, about a surprise six-month-happy-going-steady party that Suzy was going to throw for me, with all the girls from Scholastica invited and the guys from Saint George too, and even some kind of a cake, with MIKE & SUZY in bright red icing written on the top inside a heart, and me and Ronny were sitting in his garage late one night drinking some beer and talking, and then we were thinking wouldn't it be something if I surprised her instead, if I got there really late or didn't show, wouldn't that be a real kicker, and then the night of the big party comes along, with me expected to drop by at around nine—just another date, Mike, she told me, we can just stay home, sit around and watch a movie on TV or maybe if the folks aren't home we can sneak downstairs after the little ones go to bed and you know what—and at eight me and Ronny are in his garage scraping out spark plugs and still talking about it and laughing, and at eight-thirty we need just a drop more of beer so we hop in the car and drive out, and by nine we're stopping by the lake because Ronny thinks he sees an old girlfriend racing down Pratt Street on her bicycle and I'm saying damn, Ronny, that girl must be thirty-five years old but we drive there anyway and end up sitting beside the beach on the trunk of his old Chevy sharing another six-pack, still laughing, and then we meet some kids who've got a football and Jesus it's a beautiful night, a perfectly gorgeous night in May, and we pick sides and then some girls come along and we ask if they want to play, it's only touch, and below the waist and not in the front, honest, and we've got some beer left in the car if you're thirsty hey come on, and I'm defensing this goon who couldn't even tie his own shoes by himself let alone run in a straight line and on the very first play Ronny is throwing to him high and hard and the clown falls down in the sand and I move up and over him and make the interception, easy, and I'm laughing so hard I stop right where I catch it and let the boob tag me, here, tag me, I'm going nowhere, I'll tag myself, hey everybody, please tag me, laughing so hard and we play until past ten when a police Park Control car comes crunching up the cinder track and this big cop gets out and says all right, kids, the beach is closed, and one of the girls says please officer please, have a heart, why don't you take off your gun and stick around and play, and the big cop says sorry, wish to Christ I could, and we all laugh at that, and then Ronny and I say hey who wants to go for a ride and the two girls say sure, where, and Ronny looks at me and shrugs and I say damn, anywhere is OK by me, so we all get in and after we're out of the city we find these back roads and we drive and drive and drive, nearly all the way up to Wisconsin, the four of us drinking what beer is left and stopping here and there to see if we can buy some more, sorry, come back in three years, they say, and I'm telling this girl who in the dark car looks like the Statue of Liberty holding up her cigarette the way girls do with their arm bent and raised and the tip of the cigarette all glowing about what I did that night, and she says can you picture them all waiting and then you don't show, and I say surprise, and then we have ourselves a contest to see who can guess what kind of cake it was and Ronny says chocolate and his girl guesses pineapple but my girl comes up with angel food and we laugh and say she wins, I give her her prize, a kiss, and damn she kisses me back, hard, and Ronny stops on this quiet road in the middle of the blackness and says hey, where do you want to go now, and I say Canada, and my girl says take a left, and Ronny says what's left, and his girl says we're left and I want to stay right here, and damn that is funny and we drive and drive and drive, and it's long past three and silent as a church when I finally get to my house.

My dad is awake and angry, worried that I'd been in an accident. They called here four times, Mike, and what can I tell them I don't even know where my own son is. When I tell him what happened he says that was a downright shitty thing to do, then he shakes his head and says what would your mother have thought? I think of Suzy's father, how I never thought that he might have been worried, and my father says you should call them right now and apologize. I say it's late, too late to bother them, and he says you're old enough now to think for yourself, do what you do, I'm going to bed.

I didn't call there for a couple of days and by then Suzy had heard what had happened. The first thing she said was when can you pick up your ring? I said hey Suzy, I don't want you to give me my ring back, and she said that ring must have cost you forty dollars, and we start to argue.

Her youngest sister answered the door, looking like Suzy must have when she was that young, and you know I bet like her mother too, clean-faced, eyes all shining, with freckles across the bridge of her nose. She tells me to come in. I try to smile to make her smile, but then her father comes down the stairs coughing into a handkerchief and holding my ring in an envelope. I tried to talk to him, to explain, but I didn't know what to say.

Now I drive for the country. A GMC truck and mostly light construction materials for building projects. It's not a bad job. A year or so after I finished high school Suzy's mother died, some crazy kind of disease that I guess she knew all about before but didn't tell anyone, and when I heard I drove out to the house. Her father came to the door and told me Suzy was out. I said I came to see you. He nodded then, looking at me. Instead of inviting me in he told me that he was busy packing to move to his sister's out East, and then he said he'd tell Suzy that I stopped by and that I should be sure to thank my father for the sympathy card he'd sent.

When we'd kiss she'd close her eyes and keep them closed, tight, and I'd look at her sometimes in the backseat of Ronny's Chevy moving down the road with the bands of light from the streetlights above us rolling across her face. And once when we were at the lake she took my hand and said Mike, do you ever just think about it? I asked what, and she said oh nothing, Mike, I guess I just mean about things.

The coaches hollered at me after that interception, like I was a damn rookie sophomore. They said I caught the ball and stood still. A screen pass, they shouted. You froze. You could have gone all the way. But they were wrong—as sure as I know my own name I know I ran. My body moved up and toward the ball, it struck my hands and then my numbers, I squeezed it and went for the goal line. I think about that sometimes when I'm hauling, and sometimes I pull over on Central Avenue and look at the red bricks and striped awnings. I think of Suzy and her father. I grip the truck's wheel, my engine idling.

# Holy Cards

## The Milk Bottles

"Children," the Sister of Christian Charity called out. "Children, who made us?"

From his fifth-row desk, Dominic stared dreamily out the classroom window. The sky behind the bare trees on Armitage Avenue appeared to be breaking apart. Little pieces of it drifted lazily to the sidewalk. Snow. A bad window, it showed only the sides of things. Dominic lived in the second-floor flat in the corner building on Fullerton and Southport, and from its high bay windows enjoyed a more expansive view. He enjoyed looking down at all the traffic moving out from the busy stop below. He liked watching the different people on the street. He was small and dark, with a swoop of straight black hair that fell across his forehead like a comma. Here in class, he had to look up to see anything.

"Once again, children. Louder. Who made us?"

This one was easy. "God made us," the children singsonged.

At home a service flag hung in the center window, blocking Dominic's way. He'd have to crouch to see under it, or else he'd push it aside. His ma would yell when she caught him pulling on the flag's fringe. It was something special or holy. Sometimes when there were no buses or delivery trucks to look at, his fingertips would trace the outline of the flag's star. Sitting at his desk watching the snow, Dominic reached forward and traced the figure of his father's star.

Sister rapped her wooden yardstick across her desk. An old woman, perhaps in her late sixties, she wore thick glasses and had a large mole on the right side of her nose and a gold front tooth. "And who is God?"

Dominic pictured the blue cover of his *Baltimore Catechism*. When he sat studying in the red stuffed chair across the room from the windows, he'd try to keep his eyes on the letters in the book and away from the sky and the streets. Sometimes when his Aunt Rose came over to visit, she'd help him out and pretend to be his teacher, Sister Mary Justine. Aunt Rose would ask each question and give him hints whenever he got stuck. After he finished his homework and had thoroughly dusted the front room and the dining room, he could look out the corner windows and play.

"God is the Supreme Being," the children were reciting, "who is infinitely perfect and who made all things and keeps them in existence."

"And why did God make us?" Sister Justine asked.

The snow outside grew thick and furious, swirling and dashing itself against the panes of glass. "God made us to know, love, and serve him and to be happy with him forever in Heaven," the children chanted. Sister then told the class to open their catechisms to the next chapter. Dominic looked in his book, thinking of Heaven and happiness. But there he saw depicted three milk bottles.

The first bottle was dark, as if full of chocolate milk. Sister Justine explained that actually the bottle was empty, symbolizing the soul before baptism, with its absence of sanctifying grace. With the holy sacrament of baptism, Sister explained, the bottle became filled. The second bottle was white, full of milk, and topped by a glowing halo. The third bottle had spots. Sister explained that the spots in its milk were sins.

"Children," she said, "there is nothing more evil than sin. There is no ink on earth black enough to portray its darkness and horror. Not even Satan himself, the Prince of Evil and enemy of baby

Jesus, could make an ink so black as to show you how loathsome sin really is."

Dominic stared out the windows into the raging snow. A milk truck was making its daily delivery to the convent across the street. All the nuns who taught at Saint Stephen's lived in the convent. Dominic tried to see if any of the bottles the milkman was carrying were chocolate. Sister Justine asked the class if sin was dreadful and if they would each renounce it for the remainder of their lives. All the children, particularly the girls of row three, shouted out, nodding. The class grew as rowdy as a birthday party. "Yes, Sister!" the children cried. "Oh, yes! Yes!" Dominic wanted to raise his hand to warn Sister about the milkman, but he couldn't see. The snow was too fast and thick. So he turned away from the window and shouted along with the others.

Then Sister told them to be quiet and to take out their number books and pencils, and Dominic forgot about milk bottles and the Prince of Evil and chocolate and spots. Next to a drawing of seven shiny baseballs he wrote a large 7 and then gave each baseball a pair of eyes and a happy smile and a curly handlebar moustache.

## The Holy Ghost

Dominic learned more things about God. He learned that there was only one God, and that Heaven lay just above the clouds. For some weeks then while at the bay windows Dominic ignored the buses and trucks and gazed up at the Chicago sky. He did this until his mother yelled at him to stop before he deformed his neck.

Then Sister Justine confused his picture of things by informing her class about the existence of the Holy Trinity. Try as she would to explain it, even by offering analogies to shamrocks and isosceles triangles and 3-in-One Oil, the children simply couldn't fathom how one person could really be three persons at the same time. No matter how you looked at it, Dominic reasoned, it didn't make any sense. From the lessons in his number book he knew that one plus one plus one could never equal anything but three. Finally he gave up trying to understand, thinking he'd wait until he died in the state of sanctifying grace and his eternal soul drifted up just behind the clouds. Then he'd see God's arithmetic for himself.

Heaven gave Dominic problems too. Sister told the class that Heaven consisted mainly of the beatific vision, which was being able to look upon the face, or faces, of God. Dominic understood that looking at a pretty face was pleasurable—he did like to look at Aunt Rose's face and one evening as a test did for as long as he could until she told him to cut it out because he was making her extremely uncomfortable—but he wondered if he could do it for all of eternity. Eternity was a very long time.

He had pictures of God in his missal and on holy cards, which Sister gave the children occasionally as a special reward for doing some difficult thing perfectly, like cleaning the erasers and not getting chalk dust on everything. Each holy card depicted a special moment in a holy person's life, sort of like snapshots in God's family album. Already Dominic had collected Saint Francis of Assisi talking to several chipmunks, a doe, and two doves. He had one of Saint Christopher giving baby Jesus a piggyback ride. He had Christ pointing to his immense and bloody Sacred Heart. He had Our Lady of Fatima standing on a cloud before three children and their lambs. He had Saint Joseph holding his carpenter's tools and a white lily. Dominic cherished his holy cards but didn't think he could look at them or at God forever. Did anyone ever look away? he thought. What happened to them when they did? What if they had to go to the bathroom? Or had to sneeze? Wriggling in his seat, Dominic was tempted to ask Sister these questions but was too frightened. He went back to staring at the sky and the bare, intricate branches of trees.

Sister told the children that when they had questions of faith they should pray to the Holy Ghost for strength. He was in charge of all of God's grace, Sister said. She showed the class a picture of the Holy Ghost hovering over the Virgin Mary's head, shooting out tiny rays of grace.

Dominic prayed then to the Holy Ghost. He felt sort of sorry for him because he was just a bird. It seemed unfair since God the Father, with his long white beard and fancy gold chair up in Heaven, and God the Son, with his crown of thorns and crucifix, got to be actual people. Dominic wondered if the Holy Ghost ever felt jealous. Dominic knew he'd be jealous if he were the Holy Ghost.

While at Mass the next Sunday morning with his mother and Aunt Rose, with the priest singing "Dominus vobiscum," and the people singing in response, "Et cum spiritu tuo," Dominic spied a pigeon flying just below the high, arched ceiling of the church.

"There's the Holy Ghost!" he cried.

Aunt Rose laughed. His ma told him to hush. But Dominic became so excited that he cried out once more. Aunt Rose then leaned over to him and very seriously whispered, "Look, when he flies near the lights, you can see his halo, can't you?" That silenced Dominic for a while. Sure enough it was true, if you squinted your eyes just right. When Mass was over Dominic pulled away from the two women to kneel and wave good-bye.

The next day at morning Mass with his classmates he kept an eye on the ceiling, and then again just after the Offertory everyone in church saw him as he fluttered off the top of one of the lights and swooped down low over the children's heads, and each of the children looked up. Then for a while he flew back and forth, kind of showing off, while the priest offered the bread and wine. Then everyone saw him fly straight as an arrow into one of the stained-glass windows and, with a smash, break his holy neck. Several of the children screamed. A few of the smaller kids began to cry, undoubtedly overwhelmed by all of the grace invisibly exploding out of the feebly flapping body as it twirled down through the air and then landed with a soft thump on the church's marble floor.

Dominic smiled and prayed feverishly. He knew that the Holy Ghost had been finally fed up with being just a bird and had decided to die like his big brother Jesus. Dominic knew that after three days the Holy Ghost would rise up and be alive again, and that later he'd ascend into Heaven. And, sure enough, three days later when Dominic checked the pews beneath the stained-glass window, the Holy Ghost was no longer there. Dominic was filled with joy because he knew that the Holy Ghost had risen.

"Alleluia, alleluia," Dominic cried. "Alleluia."

## Martyrs

The Chicago sky was as gray as lint clogging a drain. Dominic sat at his desk, head resting on his arms, eyes staring out the windows. He was counting the pink bricks of the convent across the street, grouping them in tens, then twenties. Before him stood Sister Justine, her arms folded beneath the outer robes of her black habit.

"Children," she was saying, "we learn through example." Her gold front tooth glistened wetly in the room's fluorescent light.

She was telling them the story of Saint Stephen, their patron saint. He had been the Church's first martyr. Stoned by the Church's enemies because they were envious of his knowledge and power, Stephen had gained the immediate reward of Heaven. Sister told the children that they must learn to suffer for their faith.

Before Stephen died, he said two things. Sister had asked the class to memorize these last sacred words, as they were recorded in the Acts of the Apostles by one of the apostles who had witnessed Stephen's death.

Dominic was counting the bricks around the hedges. He

was up to sixteen. Four more would make another twenty. He stopped, surveyed the back of the kid's head in front of him, shivered in the suddenly chilly classroom, and then slowly raised his hand.

"Yes, Dominic?" Sister said.

He was nervous as he stood in the aisle. He could feel everyone in class looking at him. It was no small thing interrupting a lesson, but if your question was a good one, one that showed attention and thought, you earned extra points toward your next holy card. Slowly he asked, "Sister, why didn't the apostle try to help Saint Stephen?"

"I don't know what you mean," Sister said.

Maybe it was a dumb question, Dominic thought. He looked out the windows at the convent, then rubbed his chin. "I mean, if he was there too when the heathens were killing him, why didn't he fight too?"

Sister Justine gave him the forced smile that meant she was running out of patience. "I still don't understand you," she said. "Why don't you sit back down and allow the class to continue with today's lesson?"

Dominic started to sit, then hesitated. No, he thought, it was a good question. He cleared his throat. "Didn't Saint Stephen fight, Sister?"

"Fight whom?" said the nun.

"The Church's evil heathen enemies, Sister," replied Dominic.

"Good. Now what were the heathens doing to Stephen?"

Dominic thought for a moment. It was yesterday's new word. Finally he said, "Stoning him, Sister."

"Very good. Now what is your question?"

"I'm asking why the apostle didn't help Saint Stephen fight back." Dominic could feel his back beginning to sweat.

"Saint Stephen didn't fight," Sister said. She turned and drew her yardstick from the top of her desk, then brandished it in the air. "Does anyone else here think that Saint Stephen fought?"

When she said "fought," she sounded as if she were spitting. No one in class raised a hand. The girls of row three stared at Dominic with wide eyes, wagging their astonished heads.

"Well, Dominic," Sister said, "as you can see you're the only one in the room who thinks Saint Stephen fought. Now, children, why didn't he?"

The room erupted with raised hands. "Because fighting's wrong," the girls of row three singsonged.

"Yes, girls," Sister said, "that's very good. And why else?"

No one could think of another reason.

"Because it was the will of God," Sister said. The children nodded their heads. Dominic was confused.

"You mean Saint Stephen just let them kill him, Sister?"

A rush of blood colored Sister's face, leaving a pale halo around the mole on the side of her nose. "Yes, Dominic," she said. "Because it was the will of God."

"But Sister, what about the apostle who was watching, who wrote it all down?"

"Dominic," Sister said sharply, "I think you're deliberately trying to waste the class's time by asking these ridiculous questions. You know that time is invaluable and can never be replaced. Very well then, we'll begin our lesson with you. What did Stephen cry out as he was stoned?"

Dominic was flustered. He was trying to figure out how Stephen and the apostle knew it was the will of God. What if they had tried to fight? he thought. Would God have struck them down right then and there because their actions were against his will? The boy thought of Lot's wife, how God had turned her into a pillar of salt. He thought of how God had banned Moses from entering the land of milk and honey. "Sit down," Sister Justine said, "and write out twenty times the last holy words of Saint Stephen." Dominic held back his tears, and she continued the lesson.

Stephen was buried by a man named Gamaliel in the year A.D. 36. Then, decades later, a pious old priest named Lucien discovered Stephen's body, which was miraculously preserved, still warm to the touch, and as white as the purest of snows.

Dominic wasn't listening. He sat sadly at his desk, his left hand pressed down hard against his writing tablet, his tongue sticking out of the corner of his mouth, writing over and over, *"Lord Jesus, receive my spirit."* And just below that: *"Lord, lay not this sin to their charge."*

## God's All-Stars

Dominic's mother sat in the red stuffed chair near the old cathedral radio. The chair had been her husband's favorite. Against the wall was the matching sofa, worn and pink at its edges, a pair of end tables, and a lamp. Across from her stood the oil heater. That morning she'd filled it carefully, not spilling a drop. She was good at not spilling things. She was good at numbers, at keeping them straight. In a notebook she figured the month's expenses, drawing her wool sweater more tightly around herself. It was a Wednesday, her day off from the Dixie Diner, where she worked.

Dominic whistled as he washed in the bathroom. He'd just come home from school and had given his mom a big kiss and his day's papers. His cheeks were flushed. He was wearing his new blue Cubs jacket, purchased the night before.

At the busy department store near Lincoln and Belmont, Dominic had made faces in the mirrors and claimed both his arms were broken until his mom consented to the young salesman to let her son try the Cubs jacket on. It was loose, but Dominic pleaded with her to buy it.

"But honey," she said, "it's the wrong size."

"He's sure to grow into it," the salesman said brightly.

"Please," Dominic said. "Pretty please."

"We've got White Sox jackets too," offered the salesman.

Dominic shook his head. He hated the White Sox even though they were the better team. He was a North Sider, and the Cubs were the North Side team. It was that simple.

She heard him open the icebox, then the silverware drawer. He was making his usual after-school snack, peanut-butter Holy Communions. By working the bread with his hands the boy would form the Hosts, which he then topped with peanut butter or, sometimes, marmalade.

"Dominic," she called.

He walked into the front room, the cuffs of his new jacket hanging over his hands and wet from when he'd washed.

"Dominic," she asked, "what's this?"

She held up his religion test. He'd received a 70. Marked with large red checks were the answers DEE FONDY, HANK SAUER, and ERNIE BANKS.

"Dominic," she said again.

His mouth was full of Communion. He chewed slowly and raised one finger to ask her to wait. Then he ran into his bedroom and returned with his cigar box. He opened it before her, sitting by her legs on the floor.

"Look, Ma," he said proudly. Bound neatly with green rubber bands were his holy cards depicting the bloody deaths of martyrs, the miracles of the Virgin and the many saints, and the various faces of God. Mixed with them were his baseball cards. On several Dominic had drawn halos or put crosses on the bats.

"The Cubs are the martyrs," he said, "see?" showing her the various cards listing previous years' National League standings. On nearly all of them the Cubs were listed seventh or eighth, in last place. "And this guy here, Saint Tarcissus, he was a ballplayer too." Dominic showed his mother his Saint Tarcissus holy card. On its back was the story of how the young Roman martyr had played a crude form of baseball with his friends until the afternoon he agreed to secretly carry the Eucharist beneath his cloak to the catacombs to help the early Christians celebrate Mass and was stoned to death because he refused to stop and play a ball game. He died in the arms of a beautiful maiden. Dominic adored Saint Tarcissus because the card said that he fought back viciously.

"But this test," his mother said.

"Sister don't know nothing," Dominic said.

"But she's there to teach you," his mother began, but then stopped when he took her hand and led her into his bedroom.

Smiling, he pointed to the wall above his dresser. There hung his Cubs pennant and his glow-in-the dark crucifix. Behind the crucifix and a sheaf of palms was a sheet of his writing paper.

### THE ALL-STARS

1. GOD THE FATHER FIRST PERSON 1st base
2. GOD THE SON SECOND PERSON 2nd
3. GOD THE HOLY GHOST THIRD PERSON 3rd
4. ERNIE BANKS I DON'T CARE IF HE'S CHOCOLATE shortstop
5. HANK SAUER right field A HOLY MARTYR CUB
6. RALPH KINER left field A HOLY MARTYR CUB
7. SAINT TARCISSUS catcher BUT HE DOESN'T HAVE TO PLAY IF HE DON'T WANT TO
8. FRANK BAUMHOLTZ center ANOTHER HOLY MARTYR CUB
9. OUR LADY OF PERPETUAL HELP the pitcher BECAUSE OF HER BIG GOOD ARMS

Laughing, his mother suggested they move his lineup from behind the crucifix to just beneath the Cubs pennant. Dominic nodded and then ran to the kitchen for a thumbtack.

## The Bleeding Bureau

He was certain his nickel was somewhere. Dominic plunged his hands into his pockets, stretching nearly horizontal at his desk. Around him, the other kids who'd received Communion at morning Mass were finishing their breakfasts, their fingernails idly scraping the sides of their waxed milk cartons. The girls of row three were chewing silently, thirty times before swallowing, as Sister Justine instructed. In five bites Dominic had wolfed down his flat egg on toast, always soggy by the time he ate it.

He checked his back pockets. Each was empty, save for lint. Then he remembered that he'd put his nickel in his shirt pocket, for good luck, in the hope that it would put his row over the five-dollar mark and thus allow them this Friday morning to buy and name a pagan baby.

Kenneth, the tall row captain, had already left his seat and stood waiting before the row. He held his hands at his sides, as if at military attention. Dominic smiled at his nickel, then spat on it. Now it was even more lucky. He dropped his lint into his inkwell and looked back at the pagan baby mission board tallies.

| ROW ONE | ROW TWO | ROW THREE | ROW FOUR | ROW FIVE | ROW SIX |
|---|---|---|---|---|---|
| Gabriel | Pius X | Stephen | Cosmas | Daria | Hippolytus |
| Achilleus | | Justina | Damian | Agapitus | |
| | | Praxedes | | Valentine | |
| | | Clare | | | |
| | | Madeleine | | | |
| | | Sophie | | | |
| | | Barat | | | |
| | | Scholastica | | | |
| | | Gertrude | | | |
| | | Bridget | | | |
| | | Mary | | | |
| | | Euphrasia | | | |
| | | Pelletier | | | |

Sister usually helped out with suggestions for the names, but the children of each row voted, democratically, the majority ruling. This year they were buying their pagan babies from an orphanage in a place called Siam. Dominic liked Siam because he knew it was where Siamese cats and twins came from. Every time the good missionary priests received another five dollars, they took an unnamed boy or girl out of its crib and baptized and named it. Then for all eternity the kid owed the everlasting salvation of its soul to the generosity of the good Catholic children in Chicago whose pennies and nickels and dimes enabled the pagan child to be saved.

Something whizzed past Dominic's face. It was a spitball, likely from someone in row two. Dominic turned in his seat and looked for the culprit. Row two made the room's best spitballs: neither too dry nor too wet. A good spitball smacked but wasn't sloppy. It stuck but didn't stay. Row two was famous for shooting spitballs at the classroom's ceiling, where they'd hang for ten or more tantalizing minutes—so long that maybe even the spitball's creator had forgotten he'd shot it up there—until it fell in the middle of the aisle or on some kid's desk or head, disrupting everything, and nobody was the wiser. Dominic tore a scrap of paper off his tablet and worked up some saliva and wet the paper carefully on his tongue, then chewed it into shape. A guy couldn't not defend himself or else he'd become everybody's target. He squeezed the spitball gently between his fingertips. As Sister turned toward the blackboard, Dominic crouched in the aisle and fired. It hit Willie Berger in row one right on the ear.

"Have your money ready now, children," Sister called out.

Kenneth marched down the aisle, firmly gripping the shoulder of each fifth rower until the kid contributed something—at least a penny or two—to his box. He was a good row captain. Running for election earlier that year, Kenneth told the class that his dad was the alderman's right-hand man, so he knew how to make government work. That was the city's slogan: Chicago was the city that worked. Dominic understood enough to know that only a fool didn't drop a couple of coins on an open palm backed up by a hand squeezing your shoulder.

Suddenly, from the middle of row two, Eddie Dymkowycz stood in his seat and made a noise like a stepped-on horse. Out from his mouth shot a stream of vomit so solid it splashed the back of Angela Donofrio's long brunette hair. She grasped her barrettes and shrieked. The first three rows emptied faster than a fire drill, fleeing the sight and surprisingly horrible smell: a cross between old cheese and the wettest corner of a flooded basement. They took refuge by the front blackboard as Eddie let loose a second column of vomit that bounced off his desk top and rained on the floor. Rows four, five, and six darted to the side windows.

Sister Justine rapped her yardstick on her desk for order. With the exception of Angela Donofrio, the kids quieted down to a reasonable roar. Sister then ordered one of the girls of row three to fetch the janitor and told gasping Eddie and hysterical Angela to report immediately to Mother Superior's office. The boys of row six jerked open the windows without her having to ask.

Dominic shivered from the sudden cold. He wanted to throw up too. He was sympathetic that way. When people around him cried, he felt like crying too. When others vomited, he too had to vomit. He swallowed back down a mouthful of his egg-and-toast sandwich and tried to get his mind to change the subject. He tried to get his nose to smell the cold, fresh air. Sister started in on something. Dominic focused on her gold tooth.

"As we wait for the custodian, children, let's continue our unit on the Holy Eucharist and perhaps use this event as a lesson. Let me tell you a true story. There once was a boy who received Holy Communion in the state of mortal sin. Too weak to defend his faith, he ate meat one Friday with his Protestant friends. Then he committed the grave sin of pride and thought it didn't matter. Well, it did! After leaving the Communion rail, just like our Edward he vomited. You see, children, Jesus does not like entering an unclean soul, just as you or I would not like going into a dirty house."

The janitor came to the classroom door wheeling before him a bucket and a mop, and carrying a broom and a bag of sawdust.

"Children," Sister continued, "here's another true story I know, about a bad boy who purposely bit into the Host. He was angry at Jesus for some petty reason. Well, his mouth immediately filled with Christ's blood, and in his shame he swallowed much of it. Then he fell sick and vomited, and only after the blessed sacrament of confession was the boy well again."

As the janitor mopped up what he could, the children shuffled back to their seats.

"A very curious child once walked to the back of the church and spat the Eucharist into his handkerchief and foolishly took it home, then further desecrated it by hiding it in his dresser drawer. What could this boy have been thinking? Did he think he could contain Christ? By dawn the next morning, his bureau drawer overflowed with blood! It got on his hands and face, and when the boy tried to wipe it off it couldn't be removed! The little sinner then tried to staunch its flow, but no tourniquet save the prayers of an anointed priest could stem the flood of blood gushing from the drawer."

The janitor slowly spread the sawdust.

"Now children, I certainly don't intend to say that either Edward or Angela did any of these things, but I do want to impress upon each of you that God is supremely powerful, and that he works in many strange and mysterious ways!"

Dominic swallowed hard as he stared at a spot on his desk top. He pictured his own bureau gushing with blood, his mother's disappointment, the monsignor's angry face, Aunt Rose's sadness. During the next moment, as a spitball plopped on his desk, he imagined the crucified Christ's extraordinary pain and Satan's simultaneous glee. Dominic shuddered. His pants flowed hot and wet.

As soon as he realized what he'd done, he began crying. No one yet noticed the puddle beneath his desk, so he slowly raised his hand.

When Sister moved on to another story—this one about a bad boy who impaled a stolen Host upon a nail—Dominic stood and covered the front of his pants with his hands and made his way down his row, past a kid picking his nose, a girl copying her spelling words in neat Palmer cursive, a boy playing paper-puck hockey with his pencil and inkwell, Kenneth counting the row's nickels and dimes.

"Dominic," Sister called, "return to your seat at once."

He knew that she'd discover his accident in another minute, so he made his way to Mother Superior's office without waiting to be told. He didn't turn. Peeing was bad enough. He didn't want the whole class to see his tears too.

## Nativity

The cathedral radio played a medley of church songs.

"Wear two pairs of socks," his mother called. She was untangling a string of Christmas tree lights at the table in the dining room. Around her were the cardboard boxes in which she stored their holiday things. Already she'd unpacked the wooden manger and a few of their glass ornaments. The figure of the lame shepherd boy carrying a lamb across his shoulders lay in a loose fold of tissue paper. The other figures were still in their boxes, waiting for Dominic to unwrap them and put them in place. Since he was old enough to understand Christmas, she let the boy set up their manger. It was a tradition. She believed in traditions. She could hear her son in his bedroom singing along with the radio. Then the boy's singing stopped.

"Everything stinks," he shouted.

"What?" she said. She walked to the radio and turned it down, then tucked her hands under her arms.

Dominic was trying to open his bedroom window. Beyond the glass it was snowing so thickly that he couldn't make out the lights of the tavern directly across the street. On his bed were his good winter clothes.

"Poison gas," Dominic said. He held his neck and coughed.

His mother laughed. "Take the mothballs out of your pockets, smart guy," she said. Dominic laughed too, then carried the heavy jacket into the front room.

"I'll do it out here with the music," he said.

His mother gathered the lights from the table and sat across from him on the sofa. Dominic took his father's chair.

"When I was a girl," his mother said, "we waited and bought our tree on Christmas Eve. We were poor, and trees were cheaper then." She held up the string of multicolored lights.

Dominic held several mothballs. "Ma," he said, "are we poor?"

The woman smiled. "Well," she said, "are you ever hungry? Or cold? Or do you have to wear rags to school?"

"No," he said.

"Do you have a warm place at night to sleep?"

He nodded.

"Then we're not poor."

"Well," he said, "are we rich then?"

"We don't have money to burn, if that's what you mean," his mother said. She was staring at the radio that was between them.

Dominic laughed. He thought that was pretty funny. "You can't burn nickels or dimes," he said. He put the mothballs on the floor in front of the radio and faced his mother and wiped his hands.

His mother laughed too, then gazed down at the rug. "You know, when I was a little girl, once on Christmas day my father gave me three pennies." She turned and plugged in the string of lights. Dominic gasped. The soft glowing lights made her appear so beautiful. "My pa said that one penny was for the old year, one for the new, and the third"—she stared at him for a moment—"the third penny was for something very special." She smiled, brushing back from her face her long auburn hair. "It was a joke, honey. We were very poor. But you and me, we're a different story. Don't we have enough?" She unplugged the lights and stood.

"Sure," Dominic said. "Three cents is enough."

Outside, the large snowflakes veiled even the streetlights. Mounds of snow grew on window ledges and in doorways, gathered heavily on the tops of awnings, covering the green metal hoods over the traffic lights and the street side of the parking meters. The traffic on Fullerton Avenue moved slowly, muffled into near silence by the thick snow. Dominic's mother took big steps. The boy's heart raced in his chest.

They walked west up Fullerton Avenue past Tartaglia's grocery and fresh meats to the vacant lot between the Jewish bakery and Zileski's shoe store. Bright lights were strung from wooden poles. The lot resembled a pine forest. Knots of people warmed themselves around fires in oil-drum garbage cans. Orange sparks flew eagerly into the air. An old man with a cane and a large black dog sat silently inside a dark shed.

"Stay close by me now," Dominic's mother told him.

He held her arm as they looked at the trees and helped her when she pulled one out and inspected it. Most of them, she said, were too expensive or not full enough or had the wrong kind of needles. Dominic filled his nose with their exciting smell.

"We used to get a tree for twenty cents," she said, shaking her head. "And look, they want three dollars."

"Why don't we wait until next week?" Dominic asked. He remembered the story she'd told him. Next week was Christmas Eve.

"Because we don't have to," she said. She shook her head, then led her son to one of the fires. Dominic spread his hands over the warm flames.

"They'd send me because I was the littlest," she said. "You don't remember them, do you?"

Dominic said no. He didn't realize he had grandparents.

"Of course your Aunt Rose would come with me too, to help me carry the tree home, but I had to go into the lot all by myself. You see, Dominic, the men sold them the cheapest to the smallest children."

His mother's face glowed in the fire.

"The children would gather outside the lot, and then, just after midnight, after the church bells rang out, the men would throw them all the leftover trees. You could get hurt if you weren't careful. We did that for a few years, Rose and me, when we didn't have any money, but when we had a few pennies they'd send me into the lot."

"I can do that this year," Dominic said. He really wanted to.

"Oh no," his mother said. She stared at the flames in the can. "Once I saw a boy robbed by three bigger boys after he let on that he had some money. And once a little girl was trampled because she went for the first tree." She looked at her son. "Besides," she winked, "we've got money."

She turned and walked to the shed. The black dog stood and sniffed the hem of her coat.

"I'll give you a dollar for that tree, take it or leave it," she said to the old man inside. She pointed to the three-dollar tree.

The old man spat on the ground. Dominic watched his mother.

"That's a three-dollar tree," the old man said.

"And I'm a Rockefeller," Dominic's mother said. "I'll give you a dollar fifty."

The old man rubbed the big dog's neck. "Two and a half and it's yours, lady. Come on, I gotta make a buck."

"Not off me."

"Merry Christmas to you, lady."

"You're going to sell all these trees by next week?" She gestured to the scores of trees that filled the lot. "A very merry Christmas to you, sir." She pulled Dominic's hand and turned.

"OK, lady, two dollars even."

"Let's split the difference. A dollar seventy-five."

The old man nodded.

"A dollar seventy-five then," she said. She was smiling.

The old man stood and hobbled to the tree. The dark tip of his cane sunk deep into the snow. The dog followed him, panting a white cloud. The old man tore the tag from the tree and said, "All right, lady, take it."

Dominic's mother handed him a dollar and three quarters. Snowflakes sparkled in her hair. Dominic helped her carry the green tree.

The two were silent as they began the walk home. Then Dominic grinned and began the song he'd heard earlier on the radio. "O little town of Bethlehem," he sang, "how still we see thee lie." His mother joined him singing as they carried the tree between them through the falling snow.

## The Clock

Sleet fell as if without end.

Dominic stood at his front windows. When he looked toward the city's horizon, all he could see were streaks. Above the horizon the sky was dirty white, like an old T-shirt. His hand touched the windowpane. He was glad his mom had finally taken down the service flag. The cold rain fell in broad straight lines and splashed upon the street and its slow traffic.

Below, from the left window, lay Fullerton Avenue, a bright and nearly always crowded street. The file of autos from the east cut through the late-afternoon rain with its headlights. They made the rain and ice on his windows glisten. As the cars passed under the streetlights, their roofs gleamed with a clean, shiny splendor. The tires made a sleepy shushing sound.

The tavern at the opposite corner had dark windows lit by neon beer signs. They flashed off and on, night and day. The tavern door was made of strong wood and had a dark little window shaped like a diamond set so high that you had to be tall—grown up—to see through it.

On the sidewalk in front of the tavern was a bearded Jew. He didn't have an umbrella. Dominic could tell that the man was a Jew because the man wore a Jew's skullcap and walked patiently in his long overcoat. Even when it wasn't sleeting, the Jews on Fullerton walked like that.

The Germans had blond hair. Italians had dark, flashing eyes. The Polish looked like Germans but were skinnier. The Irish had big ears and freckles.

The Jew on the street below walked past the currency exchange and then turned north to walk up Southport Avenue. A passing bread truck pulled close to the curb and splashed him.

By turning to his right and looking out the center window, Dominic could see east down Fullerton toward the lake. Now that he was taller, the cars and buses didn't disappear behind the currency exchange. They disappeared behind the big gray building farther down the block. The currency exchange had a green window, in the center of which hung a huge electric clock. Around its edges were orange lights that rolled word by word on and then flashed off for several seconds and started over. The lights said NOW IS THE TIME TO SAVE.

He could walk north up Southport when he went to see his mother at the restaurant. He could walk down Southport when he went to school or to play with his friends. He was not allowed to walk west, up Fullerton, or east, down Fullerton. He could look at Fullerton from his hallway door, but then he had to turn the corner. He could look into the window of the candy store, but only for a minute and never as if he were begging. The woman in the store always wore the same pink dress.

Once, on Fullerton, he saw a man sleeping on the sidewalk. Once he saw three men drink from a paper bag. Once he saw two women in a parked car kissing. Once he saw a gang of older boys throwing matches at an alley cat. Once, a drunken man on their landing pounded on their door shouting over and over, "Let me in there!" They had to call the police. Once, someone threw up on their hallway staircase, and more than once someone urinated. Each time his mother cleaned it up.

Once, on Southport, he saw a rat as big as a cat run across the sidewalk and into a shady gangway. Dominic ran the rest of the way home to tell his mom about that. She told him rats carried polio and rabies. So did squirrels and dogs. If you got rabies you had to get painful shots with a long needle right in the belly button every day for three months. In first grade in Sister Augustine's class there was a girl who had polio. She sat in a wheelchair in the first row by the side blackboard. She stayed at the school for a month and then left.

Once Dominic dreamed that he had polio and couldn't walk. Once he dreamed that he forgot his address and couldn't find his house. Then his mother taught him about Chicago, and a nurse came to school and gave everybody polio shots.

Fullerton was 2400 North. The way you said it was twenty-four hundred. Diversey was 2800. Belmont was 3200, and Armitage was 2000. Saint Stephen's was on Armitage. Southport was 1400 West.

His address was 1401 West Fullerton, Chicago, Illinois, USA.

One of the kids at school said that on Clybourn Avenue there were people who owned goats. He said that the goats ate a million tin cans every day, and that if you parked your car near them they'd eat that too.

Aunt Rose said that was no lie, what with all of the city's thieves. She said it was a changing neighborhood. She said that nearly every time she came over to visit. That was why she'd moved north, to Addison Street. Dominic didn't know what number Addison was, but he did know that it was by the ball park. At her house every time they visited, he gazed out her front windows to see it. It was bigger than Saint Stephen's Church, and if you looked up at it from the sidewalk on Waveland Avenue it said CHICAGO CUBS inside a big bright flag.

Sometimes he'd listen to the ball game on the radio. He'd sit in the big armchair with his head down, concentrating, praying for a Chicago Cubs hit. Once he was sitting there when his mother came in the room from the kitchen. She was folding her apron. He could see her out of the corner of his eye, but he didn't look up because there were two strikes on Ransom Jackson and Dominic was afraid he'd jinx him.

Then he heard his mother say, "You're just like your father."

And she was crying. Ransom Jackson took strike three. Dominic felt bad and wondered if he had done something wrong.

Below, by a fire hydrant, he saw several pigeons. He wondered how they felt when they got wet. Why didn't they fly somewhere out of the rain? They pecked the garbage floating past them in the gutter.

Behind him, wind whistled in the oil heater. The sound startled him. He turned and stared at the silent heater until he again felt safe and then turned back to his window, shivering.

Two Poles were crossing Fullerton, holding newspapers up over their heads. His mother had taught him it was wrong to call them polacks. It was wrong to say krauts or micks or spics or dagos. Nearly everybody in the whole world had a bad name. He wished that the devil had never been invented. Dominic looked at a patrol car double-parked in front of the currency exchange. Its dome light flashed in circles.

NOW, the sign said.

A moment later it said NOW IS THE TIME.

He wondered what currency was. He wondered what exchange

meant. He wondered why he didn't have a father. Was it because of something he had done? he thought. The patrol car drove away, siren blaring, and the two Poles huddled inside a doorway.

Dominic stared at the clock's rolling message. NOW it said. NOW IS THE TIME TO SAVE.

It was seven-eighteen. He turned to watch the tavern corner. His father was dead, that's all. His fingers tapped the windowsill. Soon, the boy thought, at seven-thirty, his ma would be finished working her shift at the restaurant, and he'd be here to watch her walk home.

# Sunsinger Books
## *Illinois Short Fiction*

Lives of the Fathers
*Steven Schwartz*

Taking It Home:
Stories from the Neighborhood
*Tony Ardizzone*

Flights in the Heavenlies
*Ernest J. Finney*